THE TRAGEDY OF
LOVING JAMIE CLARKE

NOVELS BY REBECCA R. COHEN

Midnight To Sunrise
Darkness In Between
Into The Light (The Fallen
Shadows: I)

REBECCA R. COHEN

THE TRAGEDY OF LOVING JAMIE CLARKE

A NOVEL

Rebecca R. Cohen
New York

First edition, December 2015

Designed by Rebecca R. Cohen & Domenico Fariello
Edited by Jordan Axelrad

This book is dedicated in loving memory of my best friend and first love, Keith E. Pope

"I measure every grief I meet with analytic eyes;

I wonder if it weighs like mine,

Or has an easier size." - I Measure Every Grief, Emily Dickens

I have been standing here in my bra and underwear for more than an hour and it's not over yet. At least Dr. Meresh could have the decency to turn the air conditioning down a few notches. Aren't chattering teeth, trembling limbs and goosebumps the universal sign for someone being cold? This is supposed to be the easy part. The doctor said it would be just like it was two-years-ago with the low-profile brace. I'd stand still while the doctors layered plaster strips on my back and torso and remain still until the mold hardened...Nope! This time they're adding screws onto the mold to help harness the metal bars that are supposed to keep my neck straight. I am so ready for this day to be over!!

"Please try not to move, April," Dr. Meresh says as she types vigorously on her computer. "We need the mold to form exactly to your body and it can't do that unless you're perfectly still."

"How long am I going to be stuck in this one?" I ask, trying to ignore the tingling sensation running up my arm.

Dr. Meresh looks up from her computer for a moment. "Same deal as with the last one, April, I can't give you a definitive answer."

What is it with scoliosis and all the unknowns? It's always, "It's up to your body," or "Whenever your body decides it's grown enough." Ugh! And aren't Doctors supposed to give you answers?

"How are we doing in here?" mom asks as she pokes her head into the room. I had asked her to wait outside; I didn't want to be that girl who needed her mommy to hold her hand at the doctor's office.

"We're just about finished," says the red haired doctor as he smooths out a section of the mold that was starting to bubble.

"And how about you? You doing okay sweetie?"

Mom closes the door after I throw up my thumb and force a smile even though I really want to throw up a very different finger to everyone in the room and scream,"you all are ruining my teenage years!"

"Okay, the mold is just about hardened," says the nurse, who hasn't smiled since we've been here. "We're going to remove it now."

The flat-lipped nurse and the fire-haired doctor place their fingers beneath my armpits and begin to extract my body from behind the brace. Plaster and glue tug at my skin as the air gusts through the empty spaces between the mold and me. If my skin could talk it would let out a big sigh as the weight of the sticky plaster finally lifts.I feel like I've lost 100 pounds and can't remember how to walk without a weight dragging me down. I think I now know how astronauts feel when they remove those insanely restrictive suits.

Drop it. Drop it. Drop it. I plead silently as the doctor and the nurse exit the room with my new back brace,bars and all about to be screwed on.The door slams behind them leaving Dr. Meresh and me alone in the icebox of her office.

"You can get dressed now, April," Dr. Meresh says. "Shall we ask your mother to come back inside or would you rather meet her out in the waiting room?"

"Waiting room," I reply as I slide back into my favorite purple sundress. This is probably the last time in the next couple of years I'll be able to wear it. I doubt I'll want to wear any revealing clothing once I have those bars wrapped around my neck. " Am I going to have to wear it through graduation?"

With a sigh Dr. Meresh walks over to me, and places her hand on my shoulder. I can already tell I am not going to like the answer.

"I'm sorry, April, but about 85% of my patients usually remain in the high-profile brace for at least two to three years."

My stomach sinks to my feet and my heart thuds against my chest ready to leap out and smash into pieces on the floor. "Two to three years! I can't go on that long looking like some creature from a Syfy movie! Why is this happening to me?"

"I know this isn't easy, April," Dr. Meresh says pulling me into a hug, "and I wish I had a better answer for you. But you will get through it. At least now you know what you're up against so the hard part is over."

No, the hard part isn't over until I get the hell out of high school and away from this brace! I should have had the surgery, then at least it would be over and done with.

2

I pull my "clunker," as dad calls my car, into the parking lot of Perkins Harbor High School at 7:45 A.M. fifteen minutes before the first bell. I make a sharp turn into one of the empty spots and nearly collide with the car next to me. My car spits and chokes as I put it into park. Geez, I used to be a really good driver but over the last two weeks my driving skills have severely declined. Dr. Meresh said that my mobility might be compromised due to the unusual design of my new back brace but that it shouldn't affect my day-to-day life too much. Yeah except for my inevitable new nickname "Hey Hunchback!"

I smooth out my salmon skirt, which is the only skirt that fits over the brace, to make sure I am free of crumbs from the pop tart I just finished and prepare for a new school year.

"Ape!" Amber shouts as she runs toward me from across the parking lot. "Oh my God April, did you see the new kid? He's so dreamy."

"No Amber, considering I literally just got out of my car, I did not," I reply, as I yank my bag out from under the seat.

That's something Amber and I don't have in common. It's not that I don't enjoy boys, I just don't focus on them the way Amber does. "I know you think boys are put on earth to be our playthings, Amber, but honestly, what guy is going to want to play with a girl with a plastic hunch and a metal barricade sticking out of her neck," I say, tugging onto the metal bars around my neck. Amber frowns.

"I saw him when I pulled in," she says, crossing her hands over her heart. "He's beautiful. I tried to park next to him so I could get a better look but some stupid sophomore snagged the spot before I had the chance."

We're not two feet from my car and I can already hear people whispering. Some kids are getting out of their cars and staring at me. A beautiful boy, who could probably model, is leaning against his silver car reading a piece of paper. He's probably the boy Amber was talking about; he looks like he would be her type.

"Well would you look at that," a freshman boy with piercings shouts and points in my direction, "robots do exist!"

"Watch out, it might rip your head off with those metal bars!" another boy snickers.

"Hey Tin-Man where's Dorothy?" says another.

Their friends erupt into a wall of laughter as Amber grabs my hand and pushes past them. I turn and see that the new boy is staring at me.

"Screw those guys Ape," Amber says as she shouts in my taunters' direction, flipping her middle finger.

"I knew this was going to happen!" I shout. I hate Dr.Meresh for putting me in this brace and I hate my parents for making me come to school wearing it.

"So is this is how it is going to be for me until this damn thing comes off?" I punch the brace with my fist.

"Just let someone else try to make some stupid comment about you!" Amber yells putting up her fists.

I used to look forward to the first day of school because it would be the first time I'd see a lot of my friends since the last school year ended but today this building is the last place I want to be. I can hardly look at myself in the mirror without cringing and feeling like some kind of alien; I can only imagine how other people see me.

As we walk into the building Amber takes a deep breath like she's trying to inhale the scent of the hallways. "Ah smell that Perkins Harbor High air!"

"You're so weird," I laugh, dropping my bag on the floor in front of my locker.

Amber leans against the adjoining lockers with her arms folded across her chest. We haven't been in the building for two minutes and already she looks bored. If she weren't so determined to go to a college out of state I am sure she would have stopped coming altogether.

"So, I heard Megan Lionel's big back-to-school party is tonight," Amber says as a smile runs across her face.

"No, Amber. I know what you're getting at and you can forget it."

"Come on April, it's just a party, it's not going to kill you. You might even...gasp...have a good time." She pouts and clamps her hands together like she's praying in church. At least she isn't playing the best friend guilt card this time.

"You don't even like Megan Lionel," I retort.

Amber throws her hands in the air and huffs. "You're impossible Marks. Are you ever going to come out of that little bubble you've put yourself in?"

I slam my locker shut and throw my bag across my chest. "Do you really think I am going to a school party in this?" I say pointing to the neck halo jutting out of my blouse. "Especially after what just happened outside?"

"You can't hide forever, April," Amber replies as the first bell chimes. As she heads to class she adds: "one of these days someone is going to be able to convince you that you are more than your disability."

She is the only one who hasn't treated me differently since the new brace went on and as much as I appreciate it I don't believe that Amber truly knows what she is talking about.

I adjust my bag, trying not to get it stuck under the bars, and head off for my first class. I round the corner and head down the hallway that has already begun to thin out although small clusters of students still remain. I recognize a few of the sophomores and smile politely.

"STOP STARING AT ME!" I yell to myself as I pass by a group of freshmen girls who were keeping a steady gaze in my direction; at Perkins Harbor High blending in when you're physically different is impossible.

3

I'm the last one in class, a first for me, and as the door slams shut behind me the entire class turns to see the straggler. I can almost hear their thoughts as their mouths drop and their eyes wander towards the metal bars around my neck. *Loser. I didn't know Quasimodo went to our school. Oh look its Robocop.* I smile apologetically at Mrs. Honor and rush to the back of the room. I slide into the seat closest to the window.

"Good morning class and welcome to another exciting year of learning," Mrs. Honor begins her lesson.

I am very excited about getting into her English class. Everyone who is an avid reader or hopeful writer is. Mrs. Honor, a former editor, knows what it would take to make it as an author in today's publishing market. I am sure her first piece of advice to me would be to finish writing my book, something I am planning to do actually.

Mrs. Honor stomps around the front of the room like an elephant. Her rotund form force the last two buttons of her blouse to bulge forward revealing the top seam of her floral skirt. Her disheveled hair flops as she enthusiastically speaks about her goals for the year.

"You're going to read some of the best literary works ever written. From Dickens to Tolstoy, you will learn what literature is truly about…" Mrs. Honor's voice trails off as the handsome boy from the parking lot enters the room.

No wonder Amber called him dreamy! He smiles briefly and as he moves into the room his charcoal hair flops above his eyes that are so blue they could have come straight from the Atlantic.

"Can I help you?" Mrs. Honor asks the gorgeous boy in the black tee shirt and blue jeans.

"Is this Mrs. Honor's English class?" He asks.

"It is. And you are?"

"Jamie Clarke," Jamie says entering the room and handing Mrs. Honor an official form of some kind and as he does the boy's gaze catches mine and I shiver.

He smiles at me but, because I'm the world's most awkward person when it comes to guys, I'm staring at him blankly and half expect drool to dribble down the side of my chin. Now a few of my classmates turn to look at me too. He must be staring at my brace. I might as well wear a sign that says, "Look at me and my hunchback!" Hanna Tillman giggles and points while whispering something inaudible to Michael McDonwell. They're obviously making fun of me.

"Ah Mr. Clarke, welcome. You're late," says Mrs. Honor as she hands him back the form.

"I know. Sorry, I was late for registration; there was this incident with the directions and my ability to follow them. And well, long story short I almost ended up in the middle of the Atlantic," Jamie says.

I try to hold it in but out comes a giggle, which gives me another glance from Jamie. My heart thumps and I begin to sweat. I am still staring at him and now it's just creepy. I quickly bow my head and pretend to be devoted to my notes, which of course are blank.

"Well, take a seat," Mrs. Honor commands.

He strides toward me grinning and I swear I can hear a church choir singing behind him. I pat my hair down to make sure no strays are bursting out, tug on the bars of the brace to push them as far down into my shirt as I can and scoot up in the seat. It seems like it takes him forever to reach me. Mrs. Honor goes back to her lecture as Jamie slides into the chair next to mine, still staring and grinning at me. I want to look at him but I won't. I don't have a mirror and what happens if I look at him and there's pen on my face or worse. What if, before I left the house this morning I forgot to finish my makeup and I look like two-face? What if I look at him and he looks back?

"Hi," Jamie says, slumping in the seat. "Looks like we're neighbors. I'm Jamie."
I ignore him and continue to pretend to take notes even though Mrs. Honor has moved on to roll call. "Please tell me I'm not the only one from out of town who almost drove straight into the Atlantic."

I still pretend I don't hear him. I want to answer him, I want to look at him but if I do I know I am going to make a fool of myself. I don't know how to talk to guys, not really, not like this.

"Is she always this intense?" Jamie asks, again trying to grab my attention. It is hard to understand him since I'm half listening and half waiting for my name to be called.

"What?" I reply instinctively.

"Ah she speaks," Jamie laughs. He cocks his head to the side and raises his eyebrows. "I was afraid you might be mute or something."

"Oh. No, I'm not," I reply in a shaky voice.

"Clearly."

"April Marks," Mrs. Honor finally reaches my name in roll call.

"Present," I shout, stealing a quick glance at Jamie who is still smirking at me. God I wish he would stop looking at me like that.

"Is she one of those teachers who always does roll call so she can embarrass those students who come late?"

"What? Teachers *actually* do that?"

"Are you kidding? In my last school I had this teacher who did roll call every day and when someone was absent or late she made a big deal about it. Once she even booed a student who came in five minutes late."

"Booed? Like they do at baseball games to the opposing teams?"

"Exactly."

I cover my mouth so the laughter that comes out isn't loud enough to be heard.

"I can't imagine how embarrassing that must be. I am so glad we don't have teachers like that here. The teachers here may be tough but they certainly don't boo their students. Good thing you got away when you did." Jamie grins and bites his lower lip.

I wonder what it would feel like to be kiss him. Oh God did I really just think that? What is wrong with me? He's just a stupidly handsome boy with gorgeous hair and gorgeous eyes, no big deal. Geez, I need to focus.

Mrs. Honor spends a good deal of time handing out copies of *To Kill a Mockingbird*, and explaining why we will be reading it this semester. As he puts his copy of the book aside, Jamie turns to me.

"So, April, I'm kind of new here and you seem harmless, would you mind giving me the grand tour after school?" Jamie asks, leaning off the chair in my direction. "I'd like to not almost drive into the Atlantic from now on."

"Me? You want *me* to give you a tour?"

If I wasn't sweating before I am sweating now. I'm nothing, just the girl in the back brace, who spends hours alone in her room trying to write, who obsesses about things like, The Backstreet Boys. I don't get asked to show people around town, let alone by a boy like Jamie. Amber is more his type. The flirt, the hot girl with dark hair and dark eyes, the girl who likes to drink, party and do things other than hang out with their parents watching reruns of *Friends,* someone who doesn't look like she's auditioning to be a monster in a science fiction movie.

"I don't think so," I reply flatly.

His eyebrows arch and his lips curl downward. He probably doesn't hear "no" very often. It's not that I want to say no to him but I don't want to become a punchline for the rest of the school when he realizes that I am a big loser.

"We're not all assholes."

"What?"

"I saw what happened outside. How those guys were messing with you," Jamie begins as my heart sinks to my feet. I *knew* he saw what happened. "But we're not all like that. Not all guys are jerks."

Every time he speaks to me a bead of sweat flies down my back. I have never gotten into trouble in class before but I am almost wishing Mrs. Honor will look up and see Jamie talking to me. His voice, his eyes, everything about him is making me nervous so getting lectured by the teacher would be a welcomed distraction.

"I'm sorry but I can't," I stare at the front of the room where Mrs. Honor is reading through the class syllabus.

"Can I ask why?"

"Why what?"

"Why you won't show me around."

Because I am afraid I'll act like an idiot and you'll run screaming for the hills. Because you're gorgeous and I'm a plain Jane and I am going to bore you. Because I'm the Tin Man Hunchback of Perkins Harbor. Because once you get to know me you'll wish you never asked. Because there is no way you could be interested in me… I have a million other reasons floating around in my brain but what I say is:

"I don't have the time, I'm sorry."

"Okay. Well if your schedule clears up let me know," Jamie says as he puts the pen in his mouth like a cigarette and smiles at me.

Ugh! Sometimes I wish I could be more like Amber. For once I'd like to not second-guess myself. I would like that confidence to do and say as I please without fear. I want to say yes to Jamie. I want to believe that he is interested in hanging out with me without thinking he is asking because he has no one else *to* ask. And a few weeks ago I might have believed it but the moment Dr. Meresh pulled straps and locked me in this nightmare my entire world crumbled.

"Of course I find William Shakespeare to be the most interesting of writers," says Mrs. Honor." Who has other interesting writers they admire?" As she asks she looks towards me. Although I don't enjoy bringing attention to myself, I aspire to be a writer some day and I raise my hand. "I enjoy the works of Lewis Carroll, Jane

Austen, Leo Tolstoy and Mark Twain. I have always been drawn to their style of writing because it always felt more truthful." I grew up with literary classics and the desire to read is in my blood. Before she can respond, the second bell rings ending the class.

"I'll see you tomorrow class," Mrs. Honor says.

I bolt out of the room hoping that Jamie isn't behind me but as I round the corner I feel a tap on my shoulder.

"April, I don't mean to bother you but do you think you could show me where the gym is? Apparently whoever makes the class schedules thought it would be funny to give me gym this early in the morning," Jamie says as he swings his backpack over his shoulder.

I am officially screwed. The gym is on the way to my locker and I have to meet Amber there.

"Okay," I reply and start toward the gym without turning around to make sure he's following.

"Have you lived here your whole life?" Jamie asks.

"Yes," I reply. "Most people who live here have lived here their entire lives."

"I never thought that I would be living in a small town. I have seen shows and movies about small towns but to actually be living in one it's sort of surreal."

"Living here is sort of like living in a weird reality show."

"You don't seem too happy about that."

"No, I love it here. Perkins Harbor is probably one of the nicer places to live. It's not threatening the way some of the bigger cities and towns are but not much happens here in the way of excitement."

Jamie laughs. I didn't say anything funny. Oh my God is there something on my face like an ink mark or makeup smudge and that's why he's laughing? Crap, crap, crap. There is no way I can check because I don't have a mirror. This is exactly why I wanted to avoid him altogether so I don't have freak out like this.

Don't look at him. Keep your face forward.

"Doesn't it get kind of boring, though?" Jamie asks as he pulls ahead of me and walks backward so we're face-to-face. "I mean this town is *so* small I can't imagine there is a lot to do."

"It can be if you don't have any hobbies or things to keep it interesting."

This is why I should have kept my mouth shut. Remember the dumb things I was so afraid of saying? Well, this would be one of them because now he is going to ask me what my hobbies are and let's face it, telling a boy you're obsessed with a boy band isn't exactly a turn on.

"Hobbies? Like what?" Jamie asks, surprise, surprise.

"Nothing special," I reply as we reach the gym. "I'm pretty boring."

The hallway is flooded with students some of whom stare at us as they brush by. We're on display and now everyone will witness my stupidity.

Jamie smiles and cocks his head to the side. "People who call themselves boring are anything but, April." I think if he asked Amber she would say I am. "Somehow I doubt you're boring."

I glance down the hall to plan my escape and coming right toward us are the two freshman boys from this morning. "Well, here is the gym, obviously. So…enjoy."

I start to back away ….."Hunchback" the pierced freshman shouts from down the hall. "You haven't returned to Notre Dame?"

Jamie's eyes dart in the boy's direction. His lips flatten and his brows furrow. "The only hunch is on your dick, turd," says Jamie as he steps towards them with his fists clenched.

The freshmen rush off chuckling to themselves and disappear around the corner.

"Are you okay?" Jamie asks turning toward me. "I nod. My head is pounding and my arms are trembling. I am used to Amber coming to my defense but I've barely said ten words to Jamie and yet he was ready to beat the hell out of those kids.

"I've got to go," I stammer as I start to walk away.

"Wait, seriously, are you sure you're okay?" Jamie asks.

I smile and nod as I head down the hallway toward my locker. I've never had a guy come to my defense before especially not one I just met. I want to get out of here and find Amber.

"I'm fine," I shout.

"April," Jamie starts but I raise my hand for him to stop.

"I promise. I'm good. You think I can't handle a couple of freshmen boys making immature jokes at my expense? I've heard it all before."

What a load of crap. This is what I was afraid of when I first became bound to this brace, but I didn't expect it to hurt as much. I want to crawl under my covers and stay there until Dr. Meresh tells me I no longer have to wear this cage.

"Well, then I think you're stronger than those guys realize, April Marks!" He winks at me and disappears into the gym.

4

I run through the wave of students rushing to get to their next classes. I feel like I'm running through an obstacle course of book bags and bodies.

"Hey, watch it!" says one tall blond girl as I breeze by her and accidentally knock into her.

"Sorry!" I shout as I continue to make my way through the sea of students. I see Amber at the end of the hall digging through her locker. I push past the remainder of students in my way and I'm panting by the time I reach her.

"Damn Ape, where's the fire?" Amber says as she shoves a few books into her locker.

"Jamie. That's the new boy you were talking about. I met him, he's gorgeous and he wants to hang out with me, but obviously I said no," I blurt out louder than I had wanted and Charlie Hanss, who happens to be passing by with a group of friends, gives me a playful wink.

Amber grabs me by the shoulders and shakes me. "What! Are you serious? What's he like? Is he as beautiful as I thought? And why the hell would you say no!" Amber says excitedly.

"Charlie heard me! I feel bad now," I say to Amber, who scoffs.

"Who cares, Ape, he's your ex and that was in middle school."

Amber is right about Charlie, but I still have guilt for hurting him the way I did. We had a messy break up and didn't speak for almost a year but what could I do? He was always way more into me than I ever was into him.

"Why did you say no? Did you have a stroke or something?" Amber asks, as she zips her bag closed.

"Shh! Keep your voice down, I don't want the entire school knowing my business."

She slams her locker shut and grabs my arm with her free hand and pulls me down the hall toward the only class the three of us have together, Science. She's practically buzzing. Amber has always found my love life, or lack thereof, more interesting than her own.

"No, I didn't have a stroke," I reply as we enter the empty classroom, which is three rows of desk chairs, a chalkboard and a wooden desk up front for the teachers, an American flag hanging over the door and fluorescent ceiling lights that constantly flicker.

Some of the rooms at Perkins are so similar that if you accidentally walk into the wrong class you wouldn't know it until the teacher began his or her lesson (yes, I have done this a few times before).

"Then why would you say no? He's beautiful and he seems normal enough," Amber whines as she slides into the desk chair next me.

"Because, why would he want me, of all people, to show him around?"

"Oh God here we go!" Amber waves a fist in the air.

"Excuse me?" I cross my arms and stand facing her.

Amber, always being dramatic, slaps her hand against her forehead and proceeds to bang it on the desk.

"You always do this. Every time a guy expresses any interest in you, you run the opposite direction. You second guess yourself and think he's only asking out of pity or on a dare or something."

Even though she's right, I play dumb. "What are you talking about? I don't do that."

"Oh come on, April, you do too and you know it. Need I bring up Kyle Wells? He obviously liked you. He followed you everywhere and asked you out almost every day but you refused to believe it so you turned him down and then what happened? He moved and you lived with the regret of saying no for almost a year. Do you really want to make the same mistake again?"

"Come on. Look at me. There is no way he is remotely interested."

Amber is using her wispy serious voice, something I'm not used to. "Why, because you have to wear a back brace?"

"Come on, Ape, be realistic," Amber says, as she pulls her copy of *Science: A Beginning,* out of her bag.

"I am being realistic. It is all I have been since my brace was upgraded."

When Dr. Meresh showed me the new, "high-profile," brace for the first time and explained how it would work I "realistically" realized this new brace wouldn't be as easy to hide as the last one, the one without this neck halo. I've been realistic since a little boy in town pointed at me and said to his mother, "Mommy, what's wrong with that girl?"

"There's no way, Amber. Especially not after what those freshman boys said right in front of him."

Amber throws her hand up and her eyes bug out of her head more than they already do. "Whoa! Those jerks said something to you again? I swear I am going to kick their little asses!"

I giggle. "That's exactly what I had to stop Jamie from doing." Amber grabs my arm and slaps it until it stings. "Ouch! What the hell?"

"You're telling me the hot, gorgeous, new boy came to your rescue like a Disney prince and you still said no to hanging out?" Now Amber is not going to let it go. "Oh. My. God. Ape. He didn't ask you to sleep with him, he asked you to show him around.

Besides if you don't go I will make you listen to a 24-hour N'sync marathon."

No! Not N'sync! I have been loyal to the Backstreet Boys ever since mom took me to see them in concert a few years ago. She had won tickets from our local radio station and thought I could use the pick-me-up. After some convincing I agreed to go and my life changed. The boys soared on stage and made me feel like they understood everything I was going through. I know it's crazy but I felt like they were singing right to me and I was hooked.

Although boy bands once dominated the music scene, the once heated rivalry between the Backstreet Boys fans and N*sync fans does not exist simply because neither group is relevant anymore. Still, I remain a loyal fan of the boys from Orlando and for me, listening to N'sync is not only against the rules it is torture for a true Backstreet Boys devotee. Amber is playing dirty.
As much as I don't want to give in, I refuse to betray my boys.

"*Fine*, I'll find him at lunch and tell him" I reply.

"Aww, my little girl is growing up," Amber hugs my arm and bats her eyelashes.

Amber Hills has been my best friend since forever. Our parents work at The Anchor, the best resort hotel in town with an unbeatable view of the ocean. Our mothers became pregnant around the same time and we often joke that we're twins just not with the same blood or looks. I mean I was born only a few minutes before Amber. Our personalities however, couldn't be more different. I don't enjoy the party scene and Amber basically lives in it, occasionally dragging me out from time-to-time and only when she plays the, "Come on Ape you're my best friend you *have* to come with me," guilt card. Amber is into sports and is the captain of the girls' lacrosse team whereas I don't partake in any after school activities, other than visiting the Perkins Harbor Library and taking out a few literary masterpieces like *Pride and Prejudice, Little Women,* and *Adventures of Huckleberry Finn.* Despite our differences, Amber has been rock solid throughout this whole scoliosis ordeal and I don't think I would be able to handle it without her.

I slap Amber's arm as Mr. Marshall walks in with the rest of the class following behind him. Science is my least favorite subject and today I hate it even more because it is the class that is separating me from an hour of freedom during lunch.

The bell chimes after what has felt like an entire day of discussing how the reproductive system works. I thought this was a topic designated for senior year Health Class. I really don't feel comfortable hearing my teacher, a male teacher no less, describing in detail how sex works. I have already had that conversation with my parents and that was bad enough.

"I bet I know who you pictured during Mr. Marshall's lecture," Amber boasts as we file out of the classroom.

"Shut up," I give her a good nudge so she falls into Dustin Haines who squeals like a pig. "Not everyone thinks about sex all the time, Amber."

She laughs off my attempt to call her out on her sexcapades and pulls me through the mass of students all heading toward the cafeteria.

The clamor of hungry teenagers gnaws at my nerves and I am freaking out. I told Amber I would find Jamie at lunch and agree to show him around but now that lunch has come I'm wishing I had more time.

The cafeteria is packed and the line for food is halfway out the door. I guess I will have to wait for my day-old pizza. The room is vibrant and alive and I can't make out any of the nonsensical chatter except for the one going on next to me between Liza Blake and her boyfriend, Jeremy Klein.

"I saw you talking to Ashley. I thought you were over her," Liza says accusingly.

"I am. She was asking for the notes from class since she came late, that's all," Jeremy replies defensively.

"Oh please, Jeremy, you don't think I know what's really going on? I'm not dumb," Liza retorts, to which I have to keep myself from laughing.

Liza Blake takes the meaning of "dumb blonde" to a whole other level. But her brain isn't why Jeremy is with her. Liza struts around school like a Victoria's Secret model walking the runway and doesn't believe in waiting until the fourth date before sleeping with a guy. Although I've often envied her beauty, I'd rather be the plain girl with chocolate hair, dark eyes and flat lips than a girl who has guys drooling over themselves to get to her because she is "easy."

As entertaining as it is to stand here and listen to their ridiculous argument I am on a mission. I have to find Jamie. Usually Amber and I will spend the lunch hour gossiping but today Amber is avoiding me. How do I know? She just brushed by me and winked. She knows my mission and she is determined to make sure I stay on course. Why did I ever agree to this nonsense?

"You have been here before, haven't you?" Jamie asks, sneaking up behind me.

I whirl around and hope that seeing him a second time will make him less attractive. Nope! He makes the tray of old pizza and flat soda look tasty. He licks his bottom lip and I am wondering what it would be like to kiss him. Yeah, because this is helping to calm my nerves, nicely done.

"Why? Do you need me to show you around the cafeteria too?" I joke.

"Well, I might. After all you never know what might happen should I be left to fend for myself," he replies.

Well if you're that at risk for damage you might want to hire yourself a tour guide, which is something Amber would want me to say and but knows I never would. He nudges me and winks. Oh God, I hope he doesn't feel the brace. Since the plastic wraps around my back and torso I can hide it somewhat with clothing but I can't do anything about people feeling it when they touch me. I miss the old brace. The one without the metal bars that might as well be flashing neon colors with all the attention they've attracted. The old brace sucked but at least with that one I didn't feel like I was a monster waiting to be taken out by the townspeople. Why did my stupid back have to keep curving?

I don't want to be one of those people who give themselves a pep talk to ease their nerves but I can't help it. *He is just a boy. Albeit the most gorgeous boy you've ever seen but still, just a guy.*

"You could get lost but you would probably find your way since this town is pretty small."

I realize his question was rhetorical and not an actual question. He smiles the way you'd smile at someone who has brain damage, cautiously.

I turn around to walk away but see Amber waving at me like she's shooing away a stray dog. If I go back to the table without making plans with Jamie I'll never hear the end of it and I'll be suffering through hours of N*sync and I think that might be worse than embarrassing myself in front of the new boy.

"You don't get many newcomers here, do you?" Jamie asks, as he pulls a piece of cheese off the pizza and shoves it in his mouth.

I grab a grilled cheese sandwich from under the heat lamps and pull some money from my bag as we reach the cash register.

"That will be $5.74," an elderly lady with hair netting says to me.

Before I have a chance to hand her the money Jamie launches his arm in front of me and hands the woman a $20 dollar bill. "This should cover both of us," he says.

"You didn't have to do that," I say as I stare at the soggy sandwich on my tray.

"Sure I did, because now you have to show me around as thank you," he says as, he takes a sip of soda. "Come on, April. What's the harm in showing the new guy around?"

"Don't you see it?"

"See what?"

"These," I tug at the metal surrounding my neck.

"Yes I see them. So what?"

He isn't even looking at them, it's like they aren't there.
"Don't they scare you?"

Jamie smiles and leans into me. "The only thing that scares
me is driving right into the Atlantic because *someone* won't show
me around this strange little town."

From the looks of it most of the girls in here would happily
volunteer to show him around, they're staring at him like he's
Channing Tatum, but he wants to spend time with *me*? This is
surreal but Amber hasn't left me much of a choice.

I take a deep breath; close my eyes and say, "Okay."

"Okay?"

"Yes, fine, I'll show you around." I cannot believe I just said
that.

"I thought your busy schedule wouldn't allow for such debaucheries." Seriously? I just changed my mind about showing him around and he is mocking me?

"I've had a clearing in my schedule. So if you still want me to, I'm happy to show you what life in Perkins Harbor is really like and don't worry we'll avoid the ocean."

Jamie smiles wide enough to show teeth and I feel like I am about to melt into a substance formerly known as April.

"How about tomorrow night?"

"Sure, I'll give you my address, if you think you can find my house in one piece."

"Oh I am sure I can manage."

This is it; the moment I know my entire life is about to be seriously messed up.

5

~~Marlo slid into the brace and almost immediately she knew~~ ~~life was going to change.~~ *The brace, tight and cold against her skin, clung to Marlo like a baby clinging to its mother. She felt trapped* ~~and knew that if she didn't get out of there soon it would be too late~~*. and* ~~although there was air~~ *she felt like she couldn't breathe.*

I found my muse and this is all I have to show for it? I always hear authors talking about their muse and how once they find it they can't stop writing so why have I been sitting here staring at the cursor blinking and taunting me for the last hour? I've been thinking about this story ever since Dr. Meresh showed me the original brace. Marlo, my protagonist, is a teenage girl whose life gets turned upside-down when she gets trapped in a back brace. But in the book the brace gives Marlo the power of invisibility. Something I sometimes wish I had. "This book could be really cathartic for you," my mom had said when I told her about it on the ride home from Dr. Meresh two-years-ago. I know writing a book takes time but shouldn't I have more written by now?

"Hey Ape," Amber says as skips into the room. It didn't take much convincing to get her to come over to help me get ready for my date with Jamie tonight. "Working on your book?"

I slam the laptop shut and swivel around on the chair. "If you call debating hitting the *delete all* button working on it then, yes I am."

Amber rolls her eyes and begins digging through the closet. "If you keep deleting it you'll never get anything done. Didn't you say that most published authors say to write it as it comes to you and then go back and edit it later on?"

I hate it when she quotes me to me.

"Yes, but when you're writing garbage editing becomes impossible," I explain.

"Okay, whatever you say Ape. Write tomorrow, tonight it's all about your date with Jamie!"

I'm not even sure it's really a date, he just asked if I could show him around town; is that an official "ask out" or am I reading too much into it? Everyone who knows about it thinks it's a date and when I told my parents my mother practically flew off the couch and into my lap.

"I told you that brace wasn't the end of your social life!" Mom gives me a big hug and says, "I'm happy to see you're realizing that there's more to life than five guys dancing around and singing."

Anna and Jason Marks don't necessarily encourage me to date but they also don't discourage it. I am a sensible person and have never done anything to make them question me. They trust almost all of my choices, thus far, but they've been terrified these last few weeks that I'll lock myself in a depression and wither away as the new brace consumes me. So the idea of me going out and being social is like winning the lottery to them.

"Is it even really a date?" I ask, almost in a whisper.

"Is anyone else going with you tonight?" Amber lines a floral dress against me.

"No, at least I don't think so," I reply.

Amber tosses the dress into a growing pile of discarded outfits on the floor and continues to browse through the closet.

"Nothing looks good with this damn brace on!" I scream. "That's five dresses we've tried that won't work and these stupid bars just rip my shirts if the neck isn't wide enough. You know my mom and dad took me shopping for new clothes the day after I got this brace and still…"

"Oh stop that, we'll find something," Amber assures me. "I thought for sure you were going to try to convince your parents to let you leave the brace off for the night since it's a special occasion."

"I did, but they had a brief phone call with Dr. Meresh, who said it wouldn't be wise, and they turned me down. I don't see how a few hours without it is going to change anything other than to improve my mental state."

"I'm sorry Ape, but it is going to be okay," Amber says as she lines up a black skirt and pink blouse, which I would never wear.

"Maybe it's not a date," I flop onto the bed and dangle my feet over the side, "and I'm freaking out for nothing."

"Is he picking you up?" Amber asks.

"He's meeting me here, yes."

"Then it's a date."

I feel sick. "Maybe I shouldn't go." Amber cocks her lips to the side and stomps her foot. "Okay, I'll go. I just wish you were coming with us tonight. You would have been a great buffer during all those awkward silences we're going to have."

Tonight it is going to be Jamie and me, alone. Solo. Mano-y-mano. Nope, I can't do this. My head is spinning. I focus my thoughts on the Backstreet Boys poster hanging above my bed. Since the rest of my room is covered with other posters, pictures and musings from the group, the ceiling was my only option. I don't mind waking up and seeing the five guys, in their white suits and top hats, staring back at me. Actually, I wish they could sing some sense into me right now.

"Why did I let you talk me into this?" I whine as I throw my arms over my face for dramatic effect.

"Oh stop being so dramatic, Ape. You must have wanted to go otherwise I would not have been able to," Amber raises her hands to use air quotes, "talk you into this."

"Fine. Give me that," I say swiping from her hands the cream lace dress that she had just pulled out of the closet. Amber folds her arms and taps her foot on the ground impatiently. "Unless you plan on throwing dollar bills at me, turn around so I can change." She does.

I slide into the dress, which surprisingly goes on easily, I really thought the lace would get stuck on the brace and tear apart. Lucky break I guess. I flip my hair so none of the stragglers get caught between my skin, the brace and the dress. Amber is still standing with her arms folded and tapping her foot impatiently but she has her eyes closed tightly as if loosening them will reveal her naked friend. Since she talked me into going tonight, sort of, it's time for a little payback. I'm not going to tell her it's okay to look, not yet. I wonder how long she'll stand like that until she realizes I'm messing with her. I tiptoe over to the floor length mirror that my father nailed to the back of my closet door.

"Leave it down," Amber says as I pull my hair up then let it down and pull it up again.
Damn, she figured out that I was messing with her.

"Yeah, but I look so young with it down. I feel like I'd be on a play date rather than a date, date."

I have the type of face that makes me look at least three, sometimes, five years younger than I really am. I complain about it a lot but everyone over thirty always tells me, "You're going to be grateful for it when you get to be my age." Well that might be true but I am not grateful for it now. I'm 17-years-old but still get carded at R-rated movies. Talk about embarrassing. Who gets carded at movies anymore?

"You're impossible," Amber says grabbing a butterfly clip off of the dresser. She pads toward me with annoyed determination and slaps my hands away from my hair as she ties it up in a messy ponytail using the clip to hold it in place. "There, better?"

Sort of, now if I could do something about the plainness of my face and the metallic rods that shout, "Look at us!" I slip into the white flats that Amber has already pulled off of the shoe rack hanging on my bedroom door and physically I am ready.

"You're acting as if you've never been on a date before, Ape."

She's right, this isn't my first date. When Charlie and I were together we had many dates and we even had a first date but I was never *this* nervous with him. He was a fine enough boyfriend and not a bad looking guy but that relationship was forced; two friends who thought dating might be fun. And it was...for Charlie. To me he was and will always be the boy who used to pick his nose and then eat whatever came out.

Jamie is different. I get those butterflies in my stomach when I think about him and I was immediately picturing what it would be like to kiss him as soon as I saw him walk into Mrs. Honor's class yesterday. Everyone waits for that moment in their lives when they know everything is about to change. Whether it be good or bad they know that after that moment nothing they knew will ever be the same again. And yesterday I had that moment.

Amber's voice comes back like a radio being turned louder. Apparently she has been talking to me but I haven't been listening.

"Are you even hearing me?" Amber says as her voice regains its full and obnoxious volume.

"What?" I say, realizing that I've been staring at my reflection this entire time. "Sorry I didn't hear you."

"Good grief, April, take a picture it lasts longer."

I flatten my dress and head out of the room. Amber follow me down the stairs and into the kitchen where my parents have left out last night's dinner; turkey meatloaf. There's a note attached to the plate that reads:

April,

This is just in case you're hungry after your big date. Dad and I will be home tomorrow morning but Granny will be there around 8:00 so our house isn't a proper after-date hang out...you know how your grandmother gets. Have fun and don't do anything you wouldn't normally do.

Love,

Mom

I can hear her British accent now teasing me, "Don't do anything you wouldn't normally do." My mother ladies and gentleman; sometimes I wish she'd be more mother than friend, it can be embarrassing when your mother teases you about sex in front of your entire class. And oh yes, it has happened before. She always claims that people from England are far more sophisticated but it's hard to take her seriously when she says raunchy things to my father or worse, me.

I forgot that every year on this date the Hills and my parents go out to celebrate the anniversary of their first day working together at The Anchor. They eat and drink themselves silly, which ultimately leads them to getting a hotel room for the evening. I always protest that I don't need my grandmother to come and stay with me for the night but since I'm not eighteen my parents aren't comfortable leaving me alone. Tonight I'm glad that Granny will be here when I get back from my Jamie date. This way if it goes as badly as I am expecting someone will be here to pick up the pieces.

"I forgot about the workiversary tonight," Amber says as she browses through the fridge. "Looks like Alex and I will have the house to ourselves again!"

The Hills are far less worried about leaving their 17-year-old daughter home alone than my parents and I don't even have a boyfriend. Amber has free reign when it comes to, well everything. Her parents gave her only one true rule, "Don't come home pregnant." Sounds stupid but I know at least five girls in school who are.

"Oh come on Amber, I already know exactly what's going to happen between you two tonight. You're going to sit on the ratty old couch in your living room and watch *Just Friends* for the hundredth time then toy with the idea of fooling around. It'll never get further than a make out session because by the time the end credits of the movie roll, Alex will be passed out."

But of course, at school tomorrow, Amber will brag that she and Alex did "it," and I'll have to play along because that's what a best friend is supposed to do.

Amber slides into the bench at the breakfast nook that overlooks the backyard with the rusted swing set that my father bought for me when I was little. It should probably be taken down but I know that for my dad it's more of a nostalgia piece than anything else.

The meatloaf has clearly just come out of the refrigerator because the carrots have an oddly light color but that doesn't stop Amber from picking at it.

"This is gross," my best friend says spitting the piece of half chewed meatloaf into a napkin.

"Maybe because it needs to be heated up," I retort as I pull the lazy Susan away from her.

She brushes her hands together, jumps off of the bench and heads for the front foyer. "Okay, well we should get going. You have a date on his way over and I need to prepare myself for a night of hot loving."

"You do that," I snicker. "But before you go…final thoughts."

I twirl like a Princess showing off a lavish gown fit for a ball.

"Perfecto. Jamie is going to be drooling at your feet in no time."

"Shut up," I say and shove them out the door.

"Can't wait for all the gory details!" Amber says as she skips down the driveway.

Gory details? Please. I already know that this date is doomed.

Jamie should be taking someone like Liza out not Ms. Plain Jane, April the Hunchback Marks. We're going to spend an hour max together and then he's going to create an excuse and bail early. I'll come home feeling like an idiot and tomorrow at school everyone will be talking about the brace girl who thought she was going on a date with the new kid. I should call him and cancel before it's too late. I'll just tell him I came down with something.

I shuffle over to the cordless phone that my parents insist on keeping even though no one uses a landline anymore, and begin to dial his number. Sign number one that I am a pathetic loser; Jamie gave me his number yesterday and I have already memorized it. *Ding dong.*

Oh no, Jamie is here! Crap, crap, crap! I can't do this! No, this is too much. Help!

6

Ding dong. Ding dong.

Okay that's twice in a row. Crap!

I turn the triangle knob that my mother bought at a garage sale last week until the door clicks open.

"Hey April," Jamie says with a wide grin. "I was beginning to think you were ignoring me until I got the hint and left." Caught!

"I know I'm sorry I was listening to music and didn't hear the doorbell" I lie.

"You look beautiful." Jamie is looking at me like I'm a shiny dessert waiting for him to devour.

I wonder if this is how cannibals look at their meals before chopping them up and throwing them into a stew. Cannibalism, seriously this is what I am thinking about? I am so glad mind reading isn't actually a thing. I wish I could say that he is the only one looking like he wants to devour the other but he's not. Why does he have to be so damn good looking? It is making it difficult for me to pretend like I'm not excited to see him.

"Thank you," I reply grabbing my purse off the coat rack that Grammy gave us for Christmas some years ago. "Shall we head out?"

"You mean you're not going to invite me in to meet your parents? Are you that embarrassed by me?" Jamie is clearly teasing me but the thought of him meeting my parents makes me queasy.

I picture him walking into the living room and seeing the framed Yin-Yang poster hanging above the fireplace, the torn and stained pink couch and enough old furniture that makes it look like an antique store threw up, and him running outside screaming, "April's a freak! April's a freak!" And if that wouldn't already send him running I am sure that my parents and their "we're cool people," act would. He'd walk in and my dad would quiz him on the latest baseball trivia, a hobby dad has taken up recently, and who knows if Jamie is even into baseball. Then, mom, of course, would break out the old family photo albums and show Jamie all of my most embarrassing pictures including the one of me from my fifth birthday where I decided it would be best celebrated completely naked. It would be the nail that seals my fate and I would forever be known as the girl who stripped when she was five.

"They're not home" I reply throwing my purse over my shoulder and joining Jamie on the front stoop.

Jamie shrugs and nods for me to step outside. We make our way down the driveway and onto the sidewalk in front of my property.

"So, Ms. Tour Guide, where to first?" Jamie asks.

This is unbelievable! He asked me to show him around Perkins Harbor but I was too busy freaking out about whether this is a date or not and didn't think to make a plan. I can take him to Gourmet Coffee and show him the one place most of our peers hang out at night, but then we run the risk of running into half of our junior class, including Liza, and I have no desire to do that. I already know what would happen if we ran into her; Jamie would be seduced by her and he'd forget about me and it won't matter that she has a boyfriend because it never does. There's always Flower Cave, we can grab their famous lobster rolls and run less of a risk of seeing our classmates. Or I can play it safe and take him to The Cove. There's no way we'll run into our classmates there, not at this hour anyway.

Once Amber and I walked to The Cove after 7 o'clock p.m. just to see what life was like there at that hour and ran into a few of our teachers who paraded us around like trophies. When our classmates found out we had been hanging out with our teachers they made fun of us for weeks. To this day, Amber swears she has nightmares about it and if she knew I was considering it she'd kill me. But at least in The Cove I'm safe from the prying eyes of my classmates and worse yet, Charlie, who still hasn't moved on from "us."

"Have you been to The Cove yet?" I ask as I begin walking down the block toward the Ocean Walk, a man-made pathway that parallels the ocean providing pedestrians a breathtaking walk into the cove.

"Can't say that I have," Jamie replies. "The most I've seen of this town so far is the high school, the ocean and a Trolley stop with a red trolley named, Hally. It was a pretty exciting day."

"Oh well then you haven't seen anything yet. We also have Cally, Ally and Sally."

Jamie's face lights up. I know it's all an act; no one is ever excited about the fact that we have more than one Trolley unless they're tourists. During the summer months Perkins Harbor is a hot tourist spot, especially for Canadians. Tourists swarm both The Cove and the main part of town looking to soak up the sun and take in the beach breeze while doing some shopping. It's during the summer months that my parents work the most. The Anchor has become the most sought after resort in Perkins Harbor and usually both my parents and Amber's parent's work double hours. Mom, Mrs. Hills and Mrs. Claven work the front desk as reservation managers while dad and Mr. Hills work as hotel managers and Mr. Claven manages the pool staff.

"So tell me about yourself, April Marks," Jamie says as we approach the entrance of the Ocean Walk.

I fold my hands in front of me afraid that if I leave them at my sides Jamie will think I'm trying to hold his hand. I thought I would have relaxed a little by now but I am still so nervous that at any moment my breakfast is going to come up.

"There's not much to tell. I'm pretty basically what you see is what you get," I say tugging at the bars to center the brace again. Normally my mother helps me get it on but since they were gone by the time I got out of the shower, I had to do it myself and couldn't get the straps tight enough to keep the brace from sliding.

"Okay well if you won't tell me something I am going to be forced to draw my own conclusion about who you are," Jamie says crooking his lips in a way that it makes me stumble off the path and hug against a rose bush. "Wow it's only our first date and I've already knocked you off of your feet. I must be doing something right."

He pulls me up and as I brush the dirt and bristles of the bush off my dress I am feeling even more nauseous than ever. I must have looked like a crippled turkey when I fell. All I want to do is turn around and go home and curl up under my covers till the end of time. I am so busy thinking about being buried alive by my shame that it takes me a minute or two to notice that even though I'm vertical again Jamie is still holding my hand. He is staring at me with those blue eyes and his lips look like they've been designed for kissing and before I know it we're engaged in another stare-off. I have a thousand thoughts running through my mind but the one that plays over the most is the image of him leaning in to kiss me and me throwing up on him. I see his face full of disgust as he wipes the contents of my breakfast out of his eyes and it makes my knees quiver. I pull my hands back and pretend that I have an itch on my neck.

"Shall we?" I say taking a step forward hoping that he'll forget the awkwardness of my movements in the last few minutes.

"Okay, so before I give you my conclusion as to who I think you are, can you at least tell me about some of these hobbies of yours," he asks.

"They're really nothing special," I reply as I maneuver around a group of pedestrians that separate us as they pass by. "I like to write and I do a lot of reading. Nothing too exciting. I'm no Hemingway that's for sure."

The sun is beginning to settle beneath the horizon with a

mixture of red and orange that blinks off the water as the waves crash along the shore. It's the perfect setting for some romantic movie where the two protagonists realize they've been in love for years. They would stand along the ocean shore and kiss as the waves crash around them and the whole world would stop to give them a moment of bliss. But in those movies bumbling idiots like myself who fall into bushes and envision throwing up on their dates don't exist. Only *I* am capable of such ridiculous things.

"What type of writing do you do?"

"Creative. Poetry and prose. I guess. The truth is I haven't written a poem since I was eight and that poem was entitled, *Snowy shoe foot*. Clearly it wasn't one of my best. "

"That's so cool," Jamie says gleefully. "I must know more about this Snowy shoe foot."

"Oh no, that was the first poem I ever wrote and it was awful. I don't even remember how it begins and that's probably for the best."

"Okay well, have you published anything?"

"Yeah right," I don't mean to laugh at him but getting published isn't something someone like me will be able to accomplish. "No way any publisher is going to take me seriously."

"You never know. If it's something you really want to do then I think if you buckle down and push yourself you can do anything. Life's too short to doubt yourself when you find something you truly love." Amber and my parents have said pretty much the same thing to me but coming from Jamie it just sounds more convincing. "What's your book about?"

I shake my head. Writing oneself into a story and as a superhero with powers of invisibility is kind of obnoxious and I don't want Jamie to think I'm conceited.

"I'd rather not say."

"Okay," Jamie sings. "Does it have a lot of vampires and werewolves?"

"Why do guys think that all girls are into vampires?"

Full disclosure, Amber and I saw Twilight four times when it was in theaters but, since everyone who admitted to liking it were ridiculed for it, we decided to play it cool and pretend we hated the whole vampire/werewolf concept.

"One word, Robert Pattinson."

I stick my finger down my throat, pretending to be disgusted. "Sorry, but I prefer my vampires without glitter." I reply, walking around a family dressed like they're heading for the theater. "Besides, vampire books aren't marketable anymore. I want to write something that going to spark an interest with an agent not something they've seen a thousand times before."

"Well, I bet whatever you're working on is going to be fantastic."

I shrug. "It could be, I guess, if I could get passed the first paragraph."

"I'm sure you'll get there eventually," Jamie flashes me a smile and winks. "I always admire people who have the discipline to sit down and really write. I met an author once at a bookstore in Boston and he had these incredible stories about how he got into writing. I'm sure yours are just as fascinating."

At this I roar with laughter. It's true, most authors have these great stories about how they got into writing. Not me. I didn't have some wild epiphany or dream that sparked an idea. When I first starting wearing a brace and saw how I looked I locked myself in my room and read and when that got boring I started jotting ideas down, sort of mindlessly. After a day or two of me staying hold up in my room my parents called Dr. Klein and blamed him for their daughter becoming a recluse.

Dr. Raymond Klein has been my family's chiropractor for years and I've been going to see him for adjustments since I was 8-years-old. My appointments had always been the same, a few twists here, a couple of leg bends there, nothing unusual but when I went to see him for a routine adjustment three summers ago he noticed that my spine was beginning to curve a lot more than a spine is supposed to. So after deliberating and observing me for a few months he sent me to a specialist, Dr. Meresh. After a series of weekly measurements and follow-up X rays Dr. Meresh determined that I had scoliosis and in order to avoid surgery would have to wear a back brace until I stopped growing. It was a devastating blow since I was going to be starting my freshman year of high school in a few months, a time when you're supposed to start becoming the person you're going to be the rest of your life. I had been looking forward to high school since I was in the 6th grade but after receiving that news, high school was the last place I wanted to be.

As upsetting as it was to wear it the original brace was easier to disguise with the right clothing so most of my peers couldn't tell but with this new brace, well, I can't remember a time when I felt worse than the first time I slid into it and felt the weight of the bars on my shoulders. I tried to hide it with the same clothing I had been wearing with the original brace but it was useless. No matter how many hoodies I wore the bars stuck out like a basketball player in a kindergarten classroom. It took me a full week to go out in public wearing it and going back to school was a major fight in my house but obviously it was one I was ultimately going to lose.

As Jamie and I walk and talk I notice that when we pass little kids some of them point at me and laugh...I feel exposed out here like I am on display for gawking eyes. I see Jamie cringe and glance at me to see how I am handling it. Mist is flying off the ocean splashing our faces as the breeze kicks up a few notches. I don't remember the Ocean Walk being this long in the past. This must be so embarrassing for him. He is brand new to this town and hasn't established a rapport with anyone yet and because of me he is going to be known as the freak-groupie. Any chance he has at getting in with the popular crowd is destroyed now that he's been seen with me. I knew this was a bad idea. My life was ruined the minute I was diagnosed and now I've taken Jamie down with me.

"Does it hurt?" Jamie nods at the part of the brace he can see.

My heart slams into my chest as I stare at my feet. I don't look at him but reply, "Not really. It is more uncomfortable than it is painful."

"How long do you have to wear it for?"

"I'm not sure. I guess until the doctors are confident my spine won't curve anymore."

"Scoliosis, right? Your spine is curving like an S?"

He must have done his research. Not many people, at least that I have come across, know what scoliosis is. I usually have to explain it to them. "Yup, lucky me. I never thought going to the chiropractor would lead to this."

"April, I'm sorry," Jamie says and smiles flatly.

I shrug and walk a little faster. "Yeah well what can you do? It's the cards I've been dealt." But I don't feel this way at all. I'm pissed and feel like I am being punished for something and there are days when I don't want to leave the house because I don't want anyone to see me. But I don't want Jamie to know that. I'll look weak and Amber says weakness is an unattractive quality to guys.

"Hey, Jamie,"

"Yeah"

Ugh! This is going to suck but it is the only way I can avoid getting hurt when he comes to his senses and realizes I've ruined him.

"Maybe we shouldn't do this."

"Do what?" he asks, genuinely confused.

"This, go on this date," I stammer. "I'm the robot girl with the hunchback and you've only just gotten into town and you shouldn't start your life here being seen with the town freak."

He stares at me, stunned in silence. It's better this way, right? I'm saving us both from ridicule and regret. I turn to walk away before he can say anything that might change my mind.

"April," Jamie says grabbing my forearm and spinning me around to face him. "I'm not afraid of your brace and frankly I don't give a shit what people think of me.

Waves climb the rocks and blanket the shore. If I could put this scene in slow motion I'd have some Celine Dion song blasting. I can see why these types of scenes work though. Jamie and I are face-to-face and through his furrowed brows and flat lips I can still see he's nervous. I could say a million things right now and if I really want to I can put an end to all of this before it begins and avoid further embarrassment.

"You don't even know me," I fold my arms across my chest and stare out across the ocean. "Why are you being so nice to me? And why doesn't my brace intimidate you? Most guys our age would run screaming for the hills."

"Not all teenage boys are immature dicks, April," Jamie says, throwing a flashy smile at me. "I am not like those guys who teased you in the parking lot. I don't care about the brace. You got dealt a shitty card but that doesn't define you. This," he grabs one of the metal bars, "isn't who you are. It's is just a thing you wear to fix an imperfection. Like people who have to wear glasses or braces to straighten their teeth. It's just a thing and it doesn't scare me. Actually it's what drew me to you."

What a curious thing he just said! Jamie begins to walk further along the path, slowly so I'll follow. He makes himself comfortable on one of the benches that overlook the ocean and tap the bench for me to sit beside him. I do.

"Those guys were relentless yesterday and most girls I know would have ran right back to their cars and never come back. But not you. You continued on your way and acted as if it didn't even happen and I had to know your story."

I can't move and I'm not sure I'm breathing. My hands are trembling so hard that I have to shove them under my legs to prevent Jamie from seeing. I should probably say something but words seem to be failing me. I thought this brace was some sort of social death sentence. That there was no way anyone could see past it, but Jamie did; he saw through it and saw me. The problem now is, I am going to have to tell Amber she was right and I'll never hear the end of it.

"Okay now that the sappy speech portion of the evening is out of the way, shall we go see this Cove you were telling me about?" Jamie says as he stands up and holds his hand out for mine.

"You mean you still want to go?" I ask.

"Of course, I do. Why would you even think that I wouldn't?"

"Because," I start but I don't have any ending. "My freak out."

"I don't scare easily. Besides, your freak out gives me another reason to find you intriguing," Jamie says sweetly. "Haven't you ever heard that guys like a challenge?"

I slowly place my hand in his and smile. I'm standing here with the sunset crashing hues of red and orange into the ocean, in front of this gorgeous boy on a date I didn't think I'd go on. If I am going to do this I might as well commit. Besides, I feel like I can do anything. This must be how Amber feels every time she lands a new boyfriend. This feeling of excitement, mystery and suspense it's like watching a really good television show and having to wait until the next week to find out what happens however, I think the anticipation of what comes next is worse than waiting for next week's episode.

7

I have walked the halls of this school every day and most days I was convinced that this school was an asylum for the craziest people but today I am seeing it through a different set of eyes. I am sure it has a lot to do with the veil that Jamie has put over my eyes.

It's been only been a day since my date with Jamie but I can still feel the crisp breeze in the air and I can hear the mellifluous sound of his voice as he proclaimed his interest in me before I almost ruined everything. Is that pathetic? Like I'm one of those girls from some young adult romance novel whose entire world spins around their crush. The type of girl I swore I'd never be. In fact, Amber and I made a pact before we became freshmen that we would never let our worlds revolve around a guy. I wanted to make a no-boyfriends-before-college pact but Amber wouldn't hear it. She's never been able to resist having a guy on her arm, which has inevitably worked out for me. It's hard to believe that I haven't spoken to her since the date although it is more of an in-person story.

But if she doesn't get here soon I might end up telling the first person to look at me!

"What the hell, April," Amber says as she skips over, cradling a History textbook. "I texted you like fifty times last night."

"I know I'm sorry. I was exhausted. I passed out when I got home," I reply slamming my locker shut and slouching against it.

Amber fumbles through the stack of textbooks that have grown inside her bag. Amber is a party girl and would rather spend her time flirting with guys than doing homework or studying yet she still manages to pull in a 4.0 GPA. She hasn't applied to any colleges yet but she is definitely bound for Princeton or Harvard.

"You passed out? Geez, what did that boy do to you to make you so tired?" Amber retorts as she thrusts against a locker. "Oh my God, did you sleep with him?" She beams. She has been campaigning for me to lose my virginity for months.

"No! God no. It was our first date and I'm not Liza!"

Amber shrugs and heads toward Mr. Claymore's Statistics classroom. "Your loss. I'm telling you, that you would be a lot more laid back if you gave into it."

"Okay, Amber, enough."

"Fine," she shrugs as we pass by the cheerleading squad.

"WHATCHA GONNA DO WHEN THE GULLS COME FOR YOU? BAD BIRDS, BAD BIRDS, WATCH OUT!" the squad cheers as they skip through the hallway.

"God, they really can't come up with a more creative cheer than that?" I snicker.

"Not with Ms. Hailey as their coach they can't," Amber wraps her arm around mine and pulls me on the opposite side of the hallway. "You have Mrs. Honor now, right? Isn't that the class you have with Mr. Romeo?"

"Oh my God, my first class is the one with Jamie!"

I have been so busy living in la-la land that I didn't think about how to act when I saw him in school. I slump against the lockers.

"Dude, get up," Amber demands and kicks my feet. "What's the matter with you?"

"How am I supposed to act when I see him?"

"Like a normal human being," Amber laughs. She has always been so collected when it comes to situations like this. If only I could switch minds with her for one day. "What happened on that date that has you all weird and clammy?" She asks and pulls out her phone to check the time. "You've got five minutes before the first bell rings to tell me *everything*."

"You mean when I finally decided to answer the door?" Amber's eyes roll. "He kept asking me questions about myself, like right off the bat he asked me to tell him all about myself. I didn't know what to say so I kind of babbled the entire way to the ocean walk."

Amber's eyes light up with fire. Her mouth drops open and she drops to the dirty floor as though I had shot her.

"Oh my God, April Marks, tell me you did not take that boy to The Cove!"

The Cove is what Amber has always referred to as "the date killer." A few years ago she brought Michael Smiths to The Cove for dinner. Amber never heard from him again after that night.

"I didn't know where else to take him," I say defensively.

"Town maybe? The beach? The movies? The town dump would have been better than The Cove!"

"Had we gone into town or anywhere other than The Cove we would have run the risk of seeing Liza and the entire night would have been ruined."

Amber scoffs. "Okay, April you have got to get over this whole Liza obsession. You can't think every guy you like is going to up and leave you for her. Not all guys are that big of a douche bag."

I don't have an obsession with Liza and I have seen guys turn into babbling idiots around her. Guys who I liked and who claimed to like me too would take one look at her and act like I didn't exists so how can I not be nervous about it happening with Jamie?

"I know, that's what Jamie said, but I didn't want to risk it," I reply as I slide back onto my feet.

I pull out my phone and check the time. We only have a minute before the bell and Mrs. Honor isn't the most understanding when it comes to tardiness. I have no idea what Jamie is thinking and all I want to do is talk to my best friends about it so I don't lose my mind.

"Shit, the bell is about to ring," Amber says staring at her phone. "Just tell me quickly, was there a goodnight kiss? Or any kind of a kiss, other than one you'd give your own father?"

I shake my head. "That's a bad sign, right? If he wanted a second date or wanted to be with me he would have kissed me right?"

Amber shrugs. "I guess you'll find out. Now get to class before Mrs. Honor hangs you for being late," Amber shouts as she bolts down the hallway toward Mr. Claymore's classroom.

I wave her off like I would bat a fly and watch as Damian Webber and Mitchell Harper race Amber to class. They probably lost track of time because they were busy making out in the boys bathroom again. Damian and Mitchell are Perkins High School's first gay couple that we know of, so the school made it a big thing. Perkins Harbor gets hundreds of tourists every year and many of them happen to be homosexual. We even have a bunch of bars with the gay pride flag plastered in the windows so I'm not sure why Principal Weist insisted on having an assembly about tolerance last year.

"Settle down class," Mrs. Honor says as I dash into the classroom right as the bell rings. "We have a lot to get through today."

I'm panting and sweating as I slide into my desk chair and throw my bag on the floor. I can feel his deep blue eyes glued on me already. Jamie. I haven't looked at him yet but I already know he looks amazing. I allow myself a quick peek and I was right. The alabaster shirt with the sleeves halfway rolled conforms to his body perfectly as though it were designed specifically for him. His charcoal hair is falling over his eyes, and it dances with the breeze that has trickled in from the slightly opened window; his skin is slightly tanned, which reveal the muscle veins on his arms and neck, something that has always been hard for me to resist. I think boys have some kind of sixth sense. Like they know what to do in order to get a girl to do what they want. To drive us crazy enough to beckon to their every whim, if they're the guys we have our eyes on of course.

Why does he have to be so perfect? Can't he have one fatal flaw, something that will prevent me from feeling like the Lords of the Riverdance are holding a performance inside my stomach every time I think about him?

"Hey," Jamie says, leaning toward me.

Okay I totally could have started with *that*.

"Hey," I reply without taking my eyes off the front of the room.

"So last night," Jamie begins in a whisper. "I had a lot of fun."

I obviously can't see my reaction but I can feel it burning through my skin and in the weight that has been lifted off my back as I scoot up straight in my chair. I sort of knew he had a good time because when he walked me home and before he kissed me goodnight he had said he had a good time, but hearing it a second time doesn't hurt.

"You did?" Way to go, April. Way to not sound too pathetic. "I mean I did too."

"I thought about calling you when I got home but I figured it wasn't the best idea. I mean it was kind of late and I didn't want to come off a little too forward."

"Oh," God he's so cute. "It wouldn't have been too forward."

"I know for next time then."

Mrs. Honor shoots us an, 'I know you're talking over my lesson,' look and Jamie straightens in his chair. Mrs. Honor could call us out and force us to explain why Jamie is staring at me. Not that I would really mind the entire class knowing that we went on a date last night but I don't really think it's any of their business.

"Mr. Clarke, perhaps you can enlighten us as to why Scout is such an important character in 20th century American literature," Mrs. Honor says, rather than asks.

To Kill a Mockingbird was on our summer reading list and even though Jamie was technically not a student this past summer, Mrs. Honor still expects him to have done the reading. From what I have heard from students who had her in the past, Scout Finch is the character that Mrs. Honor obsesses over the most. She will bring Scout into nearly all of her lessons and always compares her to other characters. Amber thinks Mrs. Honor has a lesbian crush on Scout (but she also thinks that N'sync is better than the Backstreet Boys.)

Jamie looks like aliens are abducting him as Mrs. Honor calls him out for not paying attention. She gave him a hard time his first day and it didn't seem to bother him but today his cool guy wall is down. He obviously didn't do the reading, which doesn't surprise me since I'm probably one of the only people who always do the summer reading.

"Sorry. Mrs. Honor. I didn't get a chance to do the reading," Jamie stammers.

Mrs. Honor doesn't care how lost or pathetic he looks. "Well, then maybe you should pay more attention to class and less on Ms. Marks' left earlobe," Mrs. Honor says flatly.

"Yes, Mrs. Honor."

It sounds bad but I am kind of glad that Mrs. Honor interrupted us because I am pretty sure I was about to ask Jamie if he was going to ask me out again. I have a tendency to assume and you know what happens when people assume things. I wonder if Scout Finch were a real person would she have the same fears as I do.

Would she worry herself with boys or would she focus on following in Atticus' footsteps? If she met Jamie, would she be as amazed with him as I am? Mrs. Honor is right, Scout is one of the strongest characters in any of our summer reading books but still, I can't imagine that even she wouldn't be weakened by the prospect of love. I can't imagine many people would be able to fight that off and if they could, why would they?

Jamie is writing vigorously in his notebook trying to keep up with the lecture and trust me it's no easy feat. Mrs. Honor talks about as fast as the guy who does those Matchbox car commercials. I knew taking notes would be impossible so after school on Monday, Amber and I drove to the CVS in Kittery so I could buy a hand recorder. It's not much better but at least I can pause, stop and rewind until I have some idea as to what it is Mrs. Honor is saying.

"Psst," Jamie whispers, when Mrs. Honor's back is turned. He is cupping a triangular piece of paper. "April, take it."

He was not taking notes, he was writing *me* a note! "No," I whisper to Jamie. "We've already been caught talking once today and if Mrs. Honor catches us passing notes we'll have a second date-in detention!"

I'm too nervous that Mrs. Honor really does have eyes in the back of her head. He glances briefly at the front of the room where Mrs. Honor is standing with her face buried in her notes. "Quick!" whispers Jamie as he tosses the note toward my desk. I watch as it floats through the air and lands just shy of my desk. Now it's staring at me like a $100 dollar bill. I do a quick re-check to make sure that Mrs. Honor isn't watching and sweep the note off the floor and throw it into my lap. You know that fist clenching, stomach churning, I'm-going-to-faint feeling you get right before you go down the first drop on a rollercoaster? Well, picture that and multiply it by ten and that is what I am feeling as I peel open the note.

April,

Beware the prying eyes of Mrs. Honor. She'll rip your head off. So, what I wanted to say before the teacher so rudely interrupted us was that I'm really into you. Cheesy metaphor warning: You're like my favorite song playing on repeat and even if I hear it a hundred times I will never grow tired of it. With that having been said (well written) I wanted to ask you a question and it might be a little too forward but unfortunately that's how I roll. Any chance you'd be interested in going on another date with me or be interested in being my girlfriend? You'll see I have reverted back to Kindergarten and provided three answers below, which represent your options. Please initial the one you feel best fits what you're thinking.

1)   Yes

2)   No

3)   Are you out of your mind?

As much as I hope you don't pick option two or three, if you do please know there won't be any hard feelings. I know it's really sudden. By the way you look beautiful today.

Yours truly,

Jamie

Oh. My. God. I can't believe Jamie Clarke just asked *me* to be his girlfriend. Damn! Why isn't Amber in this class right now? I think it's time to freak out now.

8

This is what I hoped for when I walked into class and now that it's here I have no idea what to do! It's too soon right? No, this is high school. So what if Jamie and I only had one date? Most of the relationships at Perkins High start long before the first date and besides, my date with Jamie couldn't have been better. We talked the entire time and never had any of those awkward silences where you're both staring at the other desperately trying to come up with something to say.

After his great speech, I took Jamie to Lobsterfest, which on the outside looks like a hole in the wall, mostly because the exterior is broken pieces of lobster traps, but it is the best place to get a lobster roll. Even though I was dying to have one, I ordered a shrimp salad instead. The last time I had a lobster roll I ended up wearing most of it. We talked about everything and he even told me about the time he was arrested when his friends decided it would be a good idea to toilet paper the Chief of Police's house. "I wasn't even at the scene of the crime but I was arrested anyway when the police chief came to my friend's house later that evening." he laughed. It was weird hearing him talk about getting fingerprinted and being locked in a holding cell. "It sounds like an episode of Law & Order" I say. My stories could never compare to his but I told him a few cute anecdotes about myself, nothing too crazy. I surely didn't share my, I'm-crazy-obsessed-with-the-Backstreet-Boys story that I had decided to hold off for date number 10 or later.

After dinner we walked around The Cove and made our way to the beach. It was so romantic walking along the beach with the sand squishing between our toes and the waves crashing along the shore. If you've seen any romance movies then you saw a good portion of our date. We did the whole cheesy splashing one another with water thing. Jamie even picked me up and ran us through the waves, carefully of course because I can't get the brace too wet. I'm sure if I was an outsider looking in, or if I were Amber, I would have been rolling my eyes at the two of us for acting like we were in The Notebook, you know minus the whole Alzheimer's-thing. I'm totally into him and kissing him was all I could think about as he walked me to my door. As I fidgeted with my keys he, leaned in and kissed me on the edge of my mouth, where my lips meet my cheek, and said, "Goodnight beautiful, April."

The minute I got into my room I wrote for hours; it was the first time I didn't spend the entire night staring at that blinking cursor waiting for the ideas to come to me.

Hello! April wake the hell up! Jamie asked you to be his girlfriend you know what you want so just respond to the kid already. Stop worrying about your looks and what he'll think of you when he actually sees the brace. The hard part is over you've won him. This is the easy part. I'm kind of getting used to giving myself pep talks these days. I'm like my own little relationship coach. If I keep this up Amber will be out of a job.

With a shaky hand I spread the note out on my desk and write, very sloppily I might add, ARM (April Ruth Marks) next to my decision. Holy crap this is happening right now. Okay here goes everything. I fold the paper back into the triangle and not so subtly toss it at him. Mrs. Honor looks up from her notes right as the note is flying through the air.

"Shit, we're caught. She saw me pass the note" I whisper to *Jamie.* I cringe as she glides toward the back of the room. Jamie has the note clutched in his hand as Mrs. Honor stops in between our desks. She glances at him then at me. She is going to take the note from him I can feel it. She is going to have to pry it out of his hand though. He is holding it so tightly his fingers turn white. The anticipation is torture.

"Ms. Marks, if you wouldn't mind," Mrs. Honor starts. Here it comes. I brace myself for the embarrassment. "Since Mr. Clarke has decided that the summer reading of *To Kill a Mockingbird* was a meaningless suggestion, will you please provide him with the Sparksnotes. We will be having a quiz on this next week."

I'm frozen. I glance at Jamie who is grinning like we've just been given a get out of jail free card and I suppose, in a way we have.

"Well, Ms. Marks?" Mrs. Honor is still staring at me and waiting for my response and she's not the only one. I still haven't given Jamie an answer either.

"Yes," I reply but I am not looking at Mrs. Honor.

9

I have a boyfriend now! I swear I would go skipping through town shouting that out loud if I didn't think I would look insane. I'm not usually the type of person to be this excited over something as ordinary as having a boyfriend but there's something special about Jamie and I get those butterflies in my stomach when I think about him. I am sure that with time the nervousness and anxiety I get when I know I am going to see Jamie will fade away, at least I hope it will. One thing's for sure, getting ready for school will be a hell of a lot easier.

"April, get a move on it you're going to be late!" mom shouts from downstairs.

I am, once again, running late. Because of the brace my routine has changed a lot and I need even more time to get ready for school. I have narrowly made it to class just before the bell rings for the last two weeks and I know that one of these days my luck is going to run out.

"Yes, mom I know. Thank you for the reminder," I reply as I throw my hair into a ponytail, grab my backpack and rush out the bedroom door.

"I swear sometimes your father and I think you're going to come out of that room as a fifty-year-old woman with how long it takes you to get ready in the morning," mom says as I fly down the stairs.

Today is one of those weird days when the Anchor is unusually quiet and mom is given the day off. I envy how comfortable she must be in that pink robe and really wish I could wear bunny slippers to school. Most days my parents are out of the house long before I'm awake.

"Excuse me if this damn brace slows me down in the morning. If it bothers you that much I'll happily stop wearing it." Playing the guilt card is basically my go to for when I'm in trouble. I figure my parents' sympathy for me will lessen with time so I might as well make use of it now while I can.

Mom's shoulders roll and her face drops. Yes! It's worked.

"I made you lunch so you don't have to eat those stale pizzas today," she says handing me a brown paper bag.

"Thanks mom. Bye!" I am out of the house before she can give me a daily pep-talk. For the last month mom has been leaving me little reminders that this brace isn't going to be around forever and that I shouldn't let it affect me in a negative way. She reminds me of how beautiful I am and that people will see past the bars and the plastic and remember that I am still the same person I've always been but of course, since Jamie and I got together mom's notes have referenced him quite a bit. Yesterday she said, *"For everything we don't think we can handle we get something so incredible we can do anything. You got this crappy deal with the brace but if you hadn't then maybe you wouldn't have met Jamie. Maybe all of your brace stuff came along so you could find something awesome. Life is beautiful April, as are you."* If anyone saw these notes they would think I was suicidal.

Ding-Dong! "Damn, I am late, that's first period bell."

Today is the day my luck runs out. Mrs. Honor is going to make a big thing of my tardiness like she did when Mikela Asher was late last week. She had poor Mikela stand in front of the class and read an entire chapter of *To Kill a Mockingbird*. I couldn't imagine having to be in the front of the class and reading. When I read aloud I tend to read the wrong line or say a word wrong so Scout Finch would come out as Fout Sinch as if people wouldn't be laughing enough as is because of my brace, let's add in stupidity to the many things they can make fun of me for.

As I'm tearing through the hallway, I see the two freshmen boys who have been teasing me about my brace. They are nasty, immature boys but they are not violent. They are giggling like tween girls who are meeting Justin Bieber. One of them is holding a shiny object in his hand. And they are racing right towards me. "Hey move over before you plow into me you jerks!" I shout. As they get closer I see what the shiny object is; a master combination lock, and it's open. The boy holding the lock raises it slightly and lunges towards me. "Here Hunch!" As Henry Mason ducks into Mrs. Honor's class I can hear the lock clank onto the metal bar on the left side of my neck.

Laughing, the boys bolt down the hallway and out of sight. The lock hums and scratches against the bar. The thing I feared the most has happened. I am officially the school joke. My only solace is that everyone else is in class so no one else can see this combination lock hanging off my brace. I frantically try to remove the lock and swing my shoulder around, which forces the lock to slide toward the front of the bar so I can grab it. "Oh my God! How can I get this thing off me?" I yell. Okay, only two ways that I know of to remove a combination lock.

1. Use the combination on the sticker on the back of the lock.
2. Cut it off with bolt cutters.

"Oh please God the lock combination has to be on the back! "I say and turn the lock over hoping the combination is still there. Nope.

When I was 13-years-old and, as my mother put it, reached womanhood for the first time, I had this crush on Andrew Slater. One day when we were waiting for our parents to pick us up I was wearing a skirt and I didn't feel the trickling sensation down my leg. But my crush noticed and pointed at me and ran away screaming like

I had some deadly disease. I was so embarrassed I played sick the rest of the school week. This might be worse than that because this is happening in *high school.*

The hallway is rotating around me and my legs buckle until I'm forced to the ground. "Please someone tell me this isn't happening" I moan. I tug at the lock until my fingers are white. This is useless I am never going to get this thing off! I hear clamoring down the hall, shit! I forgot that Coach Stevens sometimes takes his class outside to the field to run laps. "I can't let anyone see me like this" I say to no one in particular.

I know these hallways as well as I know my own house. There is a janitor's closet next to Mrs. Honor's classroom; if I can run fast enough I can get there without the gym class seeing me but I'll also have to duck so no one, especially Mrs. Honor, will see me bolting by. Without further hesitation I make a run for it and leap-frog past her classroom. I duck into the janitor's closet and slam the door behind me.

Now I am talking to myself. "There have to be bolt cutters in here somewhere. I mean of all people wouldn't a janitor have bolt cutters?" Shelves of tools, paper, scissors and light bulbs surround me. It's like a who's who of school supplies and fix-it equipment. I start sifting through a few of the shelves but it's hard with this freaking lock banging into my neck every time I lift my arms to look through some of the higher shelves. "No bolt cutter. What am I going to do?" I can't hide out in here all day.

Knock, knock, knock. This is not happening. It can't be the janitor he wouldn't knock. Wait a minute, who knocks on a closet door unless they know someone is inside? Oh my God someone saw me come in here! The door creaks as it slides open and I duck behind the shelf closest to the back wall.

"April?" Jamie says as he pokes his head inside the closet. "You in here?"

What? How does he know I am in here?

"Jamie?" I ask as I lean over a broom. I forgot how cute he is. I've never been one for the floppy-haired look but there's something perfect about the way Jamie's hair falls on his forehead that fits with the deep design of his eyes. I still don't understand how I ended up with him. I lean further out and the lock slides down the bar scraping the metal and as it does the sound sends daggers through me. Go away, please."

"What's going on, April?" Jamie asks pushing into the closet. "Why are you hiding in here?"

"How did you know I was in here?" I ask, as if it matters.

"I saw you duck by Mrs. Honor's class. I figured since it's your favorite class that something must be wrong if you're ditching," Jamie explains as he approaches me. I clamp my hand over the lock in a poor attempt to hide it from his view. "What the hell!" He grabs the lock as his forehead wrinkles and his lips tighten. He pulls as hard as he can at the lock but it won't budge. "How did this happen?"

Breaking down in the middle of a closet in front of Jamie isn't how I pictured spending my day today. I thought I would come to school flying and excited to get to English class so I could kiss my boyfriend in front of the whole class. I imagined a million scenarios about today and not once did I imagine *this*. But here I am sobbing like Niagara Falls.

"Those two freshmen boys ….they thought it would be funny," I am having a hard time getting the words out in between sniffles and sobs. "I tried but I can't get it off and the combination is missing."

Jamie is pacing back and forth between the shelves with his fists closed so tightly his knuckles are turning white. His breathing is heavy and he is mumbling something but it's so low I can't clearly make out what he's saying. I can hear a few words like, "bastards," and "kick," and "asses."

"Where are they now?"

"I don't know, probably in class."

Jamie clasps his fists together like a boxer preparing for a match and grabs my forearm and hauls me out of the closet. He's dragging me down the hallway and I don't know how he's being so gentle about it. He looks like he is ready to kill someone. He has me out in the open for anyone to see this lock hanging from my neck bars. Wherever we're going I hope we get there fast.

"Jamie where are you taking me?" I ask planting my feet on the floor, trying to use them as brakes but Jamie is stronger than I am and my efforts fail. "First period is almost over. I don't know where you're going but wherever it is can you please hurry." I plead with him.

We finally stop in front of Principal Weist's office. "No, Jamie, no. I don't want to go in there."

I tug at his arm forcing him to let me go. "I don't even know their names." "April," Jamie says, spinning around to face me. "You have to say something, this is bullshit what they did."

I'm standing in the middle of the hallway of my high school with only minutes before it's flooded with my peers. I have this freaking combination lock attached to the worst-thing accessory I've ever worn, with a swollen face and lingering sniffles from the sob-fest I had in the closest and all I can think about is how sexy Jamie is right now. He's all serious and brooding and determined to get justice for me. He's like my knight in denim and cotton armor. Girls always fantasize that their dream guy is going to swoop in and save them but all they ever get are their fantasies; I however, am living it out. I am the damsel in distress and Jamie is my savior. A girl could get used to this.

"I need to get this thing off before I do anything else," I whine. "Please."

"Okay, April," Jamie brushes the stray hairs out of my eyes and grabs my shoulders. "You're going to think I'm really weird but I actually have bolt cutters in the trunk of my car. See, he really is my knight in shining armor. The stupid janitor didn't have bolt cutters, which really doesn't make sense considering they're the only thing that can break through a combination lock to get into someone's locker in an emergency, and yet Jamie does? I swear this boy gets more and more perfect every day. Although it is a little strange that he has bolt cutters in his car. I thought only mechanics, criminals, and so-called, bad-boys who like to cause a ruckus and challenge authority? I have only known him for a couple of weeks but Jamie is definitely not a bad boy.

Sneaking out of the school isn't hard to do since there are no hall monitors guarding the exit, which according to Jamie is the opposite of how it was in his last school in Boston. Jamie and I bolt for the parking lot where his car is parked just out of sight. I can't believe I've avoided being seen by anyone so far, I really thought the entire class would be pointing and laughing at me by now.

Jamie is digging through a slush pile of tools in the trunk of his silver Accord and it's making me wonder what it is he does during his free time. He tosses a few wrenches aside and pulls out a pair of red and silver bolt cutters and it's like the heavens have opened and are shining their celestial light on the tool. I am jumping up and down with excitement, which is making the lock somersault around the bar. *What the hell are you doing, April? Do you realize how ridiculous you must look jumping around with this brace on and the lock flipping up and down? STOP IT!*

Jamie raises the tool and clamps the jaws onto the thickest part of the lock. The pressure of the cutters prying at the lock is rocking the brace and I'm getting a little nauseous. I thought this was the easy part just break the lock with the cutters and that's it. Why is Jamie having such a hard time getting the thing to crack?

"I could kill those guys for doing this," Jamie mumbles loud enough for me to hear him.

"Jamie, it's okay," I say as he continues to tug at the lock. "Calm down."

"April this is not okay. They're little shit boys who obviously have to pick on others to make themselves feel better. I hate people like that," Jamie scoffs, as the weight seems to shift at my neck. "Almost got it just a few more seconds." He's completely focused on the task but I can tell he's thinking about the boys as his forehead frowns and his face shifts from pale to red and back again.

"Can you really blame them though? I mean look at me, I am a prime target for this kind of thing," I reply and I believe every word of it.

I knew the very first time Dr. Meresh snapped the brace in place that I would become the butt of nearly every joke at school. I never prepared for it but I knew it was coming. The lock cracks and I'm finally free. I stretch out my arms, because isn't that what you're supposed to do when a weight has been lifted off you? Jamie spikes it on the concrete and growls.

"No! You didn't ask to be put in that thing. You didn't ask to get scoliosis and they have no right making you suffer for it," he grabs my shoulders and pulls me in and wraps his arms around my back as his breath blows my hair off my neck.

I feel that lump in my throat, the one I've been fighting since my encounter with those boys in the hallway and this time there's no way I can ignore it. I crumble into his arms and the weight of the lock, the torment and the fear that someone would see me with it on my brace, fall off and I can finally soak it all in. Water is pooling from my eyes and I'm doing one of those hyperventilating, sobbing cries, you know one of the really ugly ones where your face gets all scrunched and your nose starts dripping? I pull back to give myself enough room to wipe my nose with the sleeve of my shirt as Jamie looks at me.

"I promise, I won't ever let anyone do anything like this to you again," he says and kisses my forehead.

For the first time in a long time I don't feel so alone in this. I feel like Jamie and I are facing my reality together and I think I can handle that.

10

I am not naïve enough to think that perfect relationships exist. I don't believe that any relationship is free of conflict. As much as I would like to think that Jamie and I are the perfect couple, I know this isn't true. To date, he and I have never had an argument but I know that it is eventually going to happen. People fight, it is inevitable.

The brace snapped in place and despite her efforts to escape it, Marlo was trapped. Panic washed over her as she made a run for the door marked, EXIT. If she could get out and onto the street she'd be able to call for help...

The computer buzzes as the cooling fan comes on for the tenth time in the last fifteen minutes. This dusty old laptop is a hand-me-down from my cousin, Asher, and it's a total piece of shit. I have to hit it three times before it actually boots up and if it's not plugged into the charger it won't last more than five minutes but until I finish writing a book my parents refuse to buy me a new one.

I have to finish this book if not for myself so that I can get rid of this laptop before it explodes.

7 p.m. Ding Dong! Jamie is here. Why is it that I always get the most inspired right before I have something I have to do? I could probably get the book finished today if I had more time. But I can always count on Jamie to be on time.

"Hey babe!" Jamie shouts from downstairs. "Can I come up?"

I slam the computer shut before he has a chance to sneak a peek at my work.

"Hey Jamie," I reply.

"So, is the book ready for me yet?"

"No, definitely not," I insist. "I still have the last chapter to write."

Jamie pouts and jumps on my bed. "Well fine but when it's done I expect to read every beautiful word of yours."

"Fine but only if you promise to be gentle. It's my first book so the writing is probably crap," I say begrudgingly.

"Deal. But I doubt I'll have to be. I am sure the book is amazing," Jamie replies. "In the meantime, who is ready for some Arnold?" He's waving the *Terminator* DVD in the air and is grinning from ear-to-ear.

A few days ago, after I made him watch *The Notebook* for the hundredth time, Jamie made me promise that our next movie would be something manly. So tonight, as promised, we will watch the first two *Terminator* movies. I have no desire to watch Arnold Schwarzenegger try to act all night but I owe Jamie and I never go back on my promises. Once Amber made me promise her that I would go skinny dipping at least once before senior year so last summer right before school started, Amber and I swam in the ocean bare naked. It was exhilarating but it didn't last long because I was convinced that some creepy man was standing on the beach watching us. It is one of those experiences that I am glad I did because I never really do anything crazy. Once it was said and done I made Amber swear we'd never talk about it again. I didn't want my parents finding out - they would never let me live it down.

"If I say no, will you be mad?" I ask and bat my eyelashes.

"Sorry kid but you made me sit through endless hours of that Nicholas Sparks, its payback time!" Jamie says and flops onto the bed and kicks his shoes off. "And don't try the whole, *but I'm in a back-brace* thing. It worked the first few times but you're pity movie nights are over now."

I'll admit it; I have used my back-brace as a means to get what I want with Jamie. If I sit for too long the brace does actually shift but it has nothing to do with the movies he picked out. Clearly he eventually caught on to what I was doing.

I yank the first *Terminator* DVD out of Jamie's hand and shove it into my PlayStation and join my overly excited boyfriend on the bed. At least it's better than the first movie we ever saw together, *Titanic*; after two hours of watching water your bladder starts to betray you. At least the worst thing in this movie is Arnold's bare ass.

I may have fallen asleep during the movie. It is hard not to fall asleep when you're wrapped in Jamie's arms and you're listening to the rhythm of his heartbeat. It was like a lullaby rocking a baby to sleep.

"April!" my father says, as he quietly knocks on the door. "Can I come in?"

I leap off Jamie and into a seated position on the end of the bed as far away from the boy in my room as I can be. I promised them I wouldn't have sex until I was absolutely ready and when I was it shouldn't be in my room. Their reason; mom sometimes makes my bed in the morning and she'd hate to touch tainted sheets. Most parents don't want their daughters having sex in their home because they don't want them getting pregnant and ruining their lives but *mine* are afraid of touching tainted sheets.

"What's up, dad?" I ask trying to act as normal as possible.

"Did you get your costume for the party back from the dry cleaners yet?"

Crap! I completely forgot. The Anchor is having their annual Halloween party next weekend and I had taken my Sexy Minnie Mouse costume to the dry cleaners to be cleaned and pressed but had forgotten to pick it up. The Anchor Halloween party is an elaborate event thrown by the resort for its employees. It is the one time of year when the resort shuts down and for my parents it is one of the most important nights of their lives. Mr. Michael Wells, CEO of The Anchor, was trying to come up with a new way to show his employees how much he appreciated them and Mom suggested an annual Halloween party.

I can't believe I forgot about it and forgot to tell Jamie. Since it was my mother's idea my family gets special party treatment, which means I get to bring a guest if I want. In the past I've gone solo, this year I can't wait to walk in with Jamie on my arm.

"I took it to the cleaners I just haven't picked it up yet," I reply, cheerfully. "I'll pick it up after school tomorrow."

"Great! And Jamie I hope you have an old Halloween costume lying around. This party is going to be off the hook! Or whatever it is you kids say these days." says dad as he pulls the door shut and heads back downstairs where he and mom are watching some black and white movie from the 1930s. Snore! My father is a nerd even when he is trying to be cool.

Jamie gives me this sour look. He clearly doesn't want to go but I figure that once he finds out how important it is to my parents, and to me, he'll be on board.

"Okay, I know that you would probably rather gouge out your eyes than dress-up in a costume but these parties can be a lot of fun and by the end of the night you won't even remember you're wearing a ridiculous outfit" I promise.

"I am just not the costume kind of guy," Jamie replies calmly.

"It's just one night and I'll even help you pick out the costume. I know this awesome shop in town that sells some really cool ones," I negotiate in my best I-should-be-a-lawyer voice.

Jamie is sitting on the edge of the bed with his legs dangling off the side. He folds his arms across his chest and sighs. "I'm sorry babe, I'm just not into the whole Halloween thing."

"But it's for my parents and it's only *one* night," I whine. "It is really not that big of a deal.

"It's not *just* for your parents it's for the entire employee roster," Jamie snaps. "And it's not just a costume, April. I am being told to look like an idiot." I never expected him to be this upset about wearing a costume. I don't know why he is getting agitated with me; it isn't like he asked me to go to an important party for his parents and *I* basically said no. It shouldn't, but it feels like a slap in the face. I also feel like he is disrespecting my parents.

"Oh don't be ridiculous" I bark. "It's just *one* night Jamie. Haven't you ever gone Trick or Treating or dressed up for Halloween?"

"No as a matter of fact, I never have and never will!"

"But I really want you to come and it would mean a lot to my parents too!" I yell.

Jamie launches off the bed. His lips flatten as he reaches for my hand. "What's the big deal, April? If you're only going for an hour you don't really need me there. Why not go with your parents and call me when you get home and we can see a movie or something."

I jerk my hands out of his and fold them across my chest. I want him to know that I'm angry and the whole concept of we'll-make-plans-after response is unacceptable. "You have to pick your battles," my mother's words of advice flop around in my head as I try to figure out what to say. Is this a battle I really want to continue? Is it worth arguing over or should I let it go? What would really change if he didn't come with me to the party? But I've already decided how I am going to handle it with the absolute worst thing I could say.

"Why don't you want to go, Jamie? Do you not like my parents?" I shout. "Because they love you."

"Geez, April," Jamie says heading for the door. "Do you really think I'm that much of a jerk? I just don't want to go. I won't do it! And I don't want to be questioned about it."

Okay this is where my brain would typically give into my heart but I'm expecting my period any day so calm and reason isn't exactly my strength right now.

"God, Jamie, it's just a freaking party. If you really love me you'll go."

Well that should do it! I have blackmailed him with, "if you really love me," and I can't take it back. I've taken the argument too far and the only way to move on now is to give him time to cool down. He is pissed and he has every right to be. It is a stupid costume, it's supposed to be fun, but if he doesn't want to be forced to wear one then I shouldn't force him to. I know it's not going to do anything but I have to at least try the apology tour.

"Sorry Jamie, I shouldn't have said that," I rush to him before he gets another foot out the door. I pull on his arm but he won't budge so I stand at his side. "I don't know what is wrong with me today. If you don't want to go its fine we can grab a movie or something when I get back, okay?"

Of course it's not okay. I freaked out on him over a stupid outfit. I don't want him to leave. People always say you shouldn't leave angry. Or is it you shouldn't go to bed angry? Whatever it is I don't want to do it. I want to fix this and I want to fix it now.

"It's fine. I'll talk to you later," Jamie says and slams the door shut.

11

"He'll forgive you sweetie, they always do," my mother says as she slides a brush through my hair. "He just needs time to cool off."

"What if he doesn't?" I whisper, afraid my father will hear me.

I haven't told him about the fight. When Charlie and I used to fight I would tell my dad and he would always flip out and say things like, "I'll kick his scrawny little ass if he hurt you!" Or "Did he try something? Oh just tell me he tried something and I'll make sure he never gets near another girl again!" The truth is, my dad is not a violent man. I'm not sure he's ever been in a real fight before. He claims that when he was in high school he fought the school bully and won, but every time he tells that story mom always giggles. Still, I'd rather not put any negative thoughts in his head about Jamie so that when we reconcile they will still be buddies.

"He will," mom says as she slips on her felt mouse ears that she has worn every year even if she isn't dressing up as a mouse, and pushes a stray piece of hair into a bobby pin. "Men are more sensitive than they would like you to think. Trust me I am sure he is having as hard of a time about this fight as you are."

"I'm not so sure," I choke back the lump building in my throat. "What if this is the end of Jamie and me? No one else is going to look at me the way Jamie does. He's the only person in my life who looks at me and sees more than just a girl in a back brace."

Mom enters the frame of the mirror and I can see both our reflections. I never realized how much we look alike. I guess this is what my future self will look like. It could be worse, right?

"Oh, April. No one looks at you and sees only a girl in a brace. They see you, the wonderful, bright, charming, writer that you are. Jamie is special but he isn't the only one who knows how incredible you are," mom insists. "Having your first fight with someone is tough but I promise you everything will work out. You'll see." Mom pats my shoulders and kisses the top of my head as she exits the mirror. "Now get dressed and make sure you wear your dancing shoes because this mama wants to cut a rug tonight!"

She waltzes out of the room with her imaginary partner and I muster a giggle. I'm still miserable but it is an important night for my parents so I have to go. Besides it gives me an excuse to wear my favorite Minnie Mouse costume. I've been wearing the brace for 23-hours a day for several months now so since tonight is a special occasion Dr. Meresh feels that I could leave my brace off for the party. It is a relief to not have the weight of the plastic and metal resting on me. The bars, although not directly on my shoulders, put a lot of pressure on the rest of the brace and I often feel sore right before bed, like I just went to the gym. I've got that whole sexy-mouse vibe going on tonight, although it would be a lot sexier with the glisten of the translucent stockings rather than the mournful vision of the black leggings. It is a shame that Jamie isn't here to see this. I have played the fight over in my head a hundred times and each time I do the more I realize how selfish and stupid I was being. I wish I could hit rewind and be meeting up with him after the party. Instead I am going solo and coming home to an empty room.

The Anchor looks magical tonight. White twinkling lights are strung up along the main business and ocean-view walkways leading to each of the guest rooms. It looks like a Christmas paradise even though it's a Halloween-themed event.

"Still no word?" my mother asks quietly as we approach the twinkling restaurant.

I can hear music blasting from inside and see faint shadows as partygoers mingle inside. Skull shaped lights wrap around a velvet rope that separates the outer patio from the restaurant. I feel like I'm entering the set of a Tim Burton movie, which centers around a bald giant. Every time The Anchor holds these appreciation parties they hire a bouncer (for lack of a better word). It is a special event for the employees and their families, not for resort guests.

"Anna and Jason Marks and our daughter, April," my father says to the burly man with a naked scalp and metal hoop running through his lip.

"Go ahead," the pierced bouncer says nodding toward the door and giving me a once over.

It is strange having a grown man look at me like that. Amber would have loved it. She enjoys being gawked at by any human being with a penis. I however only want Jamie's eyes on me.

The party is exactly as I expect it to be. There is a chef's table in the rear of the restaurant with a bevy of food items bathing in hot water inside chafing dishes. The bar back is decorated with spider webs, pumpkins and black cat cutouts. The bar houses the finest wines and top shelf alcohol; everything's the same as it was for the last party the Anchor had here. Princesses, Ninjas, Cats and a few Captain Jack Sparrows stroll about, taking it all in, some of them cradling their drinks like they're made of gold. Like mom and me everyone has recycled their costumes from last year's party.

"Anna! Jason!" A middle-aged Cinderella shouts as she and her Prince cross the sea of people. "Don't you two look wonderful?"

"Well if it isn't Cinderella Kaitlyn and her Prince Asher," my mother says giving Amber's parents a hug. "I see you, like everyone else, went with last year's costume."

"It's a tradition," Asher says shaking my father's hand. "And April, you are by far the prettiest mouse I have ever seen." He says this every year.

"Hi Mr. Hill," I reply. "Was Amber upset she couldn't come...again?"

Every year Amber begs her parents to bring her along so she and I can spend the night making fun of their co-workers and every year they deny her request. "No guests allowed remember?" Mrs. Hill always says, and of course Amber will whine about how her best friend is there and she should be with me. These parties would be a lot more fun if Amber were here. I didn't tell her that I invited Jamie to come with me tonight. She would be pissed that I didn't ask her first.

"Oh you know Amber and parties," Mrs. Hill chuckles. "If that girl could live her life in one extended party she would."

"So, Asher, did you see that piece on the news last night about the economic status of the working class? It looks things are finally starting to improve now that..." dad's voice trails off as I detach from the conversation.

"April, why don't you go get yourself something to eat? We'll join you shortly," mom says. That's my queue and I don't need a second invite to eat.

Lobster Alfredo, Chicken Parmigiana, Filet Mignon, Garlic & Herb Linguine and the choice of a garden salad or classic Caesar! "Lobster and Chicken, and both salads, let's go for it!" I cry. I may be a small girl but I can pack the food away. I lay on a few spoonfuls of the linguine." I would love to try a piece of the filet but my plate is so heavy I am going to have to sit down." I say to myself.

Making my way over to one of the only tables still available I notice the ice cream sundae bar. "Oh my god, every topping in the world…and vats of vanilla, chocolate and strawberry!" I already know the sundae I am going to be making for myself: Vanilla topped with some of the maraschino cherries, hot fudge and M&M's, a concoction that can only be completed by whipped cream.

I love coming to these parties but I really wish they would pick better music. Would it kill them to play something current? These one note tunes drive me insane The DJ is an elderly man with a neon orange button down, black slacks and a green fedora. Considering he looks like he is stuck in the 80s I doubt he will have any Backstreet Boys songs in his collection. "Do you take any requests?" I ask him. Maybe I'll get lucky. And I do! You know how in the movies the crowd seems to disappear right before the hero or heroine is about to see something spectacular? Well, before the DJ can answer me I see standing against the bar, in glistening black and white perfection, is Jamie!

As he catches my eye I smile and signal for him to join me at the table. With a gleeful leap he strolls toward me looking like James Bond. Actually that's his outfit! I shift up in my seat, adjust the headband ears and throw my fork crashing onto the plate. My heart is fluttering and I swear I am going to pass out and I am very aware of the fact that I might have food stuck in my teeth.

"Excuse me Miss, I don't mean to disrupt your dinner but I was just over by the bar and couldn't help but notice that you're alone tonight," Jamie says placing his drink on the table. He's stammering which means he's nervous too. I'm glad I'm not the only one. "I had to know why on earth a beautiful mouse like yourself is alone at a party as spectacular as this."

I have two choices, I can either allow my pride to get the best of me or I can do what I have been dying to do since he stormed out the night of our fight.

"Well, I had a date but he got so wasted on catnip that the bouncer had to haul him out of here" I reply.

I've never been very good with sarcasm or flirting for that matter. But no matter what I say it is going to come out sounding really stupid.

"Well my gain then," Jamie says sliding into the seat across from me.

It's obvious that neither one of us wants to bring up that awful night. It was our first fight and we had promised one another that we'd never fight over stupid things but that was exactly what we did. I've never had a serious relationship before and any time Charlie and I fought the fights always dwindled away like receding water after a rain shower.

"So, no brace tonight?" Jamie asks, taking a sip of his drink.

"Nope!" I cheer. "It's a special occasion so my parents said I could leave it off. I look so much nicer without it right?" I slide off the chair and do a little spin so Jamie can see the entire outfit.

"You *always* look beautiful, April, brace or no brace."

Sitting back down, unsure as to where I am going or why I am speaking, I say, "Jamie, I'm so sorry. I shouldn't have tried to force you to come to this."

"Stop," Jamie says placing his hand on mine. "You have nothing to apologize for. I was the idiot. I should have put my own stubbornness aside in the first place," he rubs my cheek with the back of his hand, which is wet from sweat. "I don't know what came over me the other night either. It doesn't make sense, I know and it didn't take me long to realize how idiotic I was being so I ran out, rented a tux, and decided that instead of calling you I would show up all James Bond style."

"Well if you ask me, James Bond has nothing on you."

Jamie grabs my arm and slides me off the chair so quickly I nearly fall. It's strange but I feel closer to him than I ever have and I can't help but wonder if perhaps the make ups after fights will always feel this special.

"I love you, April." He presses his cheek against mine so his lips are just barely touching my ears. I feel a shiver and the warmth of his breath against my skin.

"You know how I feel, Jamie." I reply and pull him in and allow the music to carry us away.

12

The party was still going strong and my parents were onto their third cocktail when Jamie and I skipped out early; and since the Hills offered to drive my parents' home I am not in charge of carrying them to their bed.

The house is eerily quiet as we enter the foyer. My parents left the living room and kitchen lights on at the house so it's bright enough for us not to trip and fall on any wayward furniture but somehow it still doesn't seem bright enough. I flip the light on in the hallway and stand in the archway of the living room.

"You really do look beautiful tonight," Jamie stammers as he strides towards me.

My knees are shaking and my heart is banging against my chest so loudly I swear my neighbors can hear it. My Jamie Bond smiles at me and I swear, he knows what I'm thinking. This is the first time that he and I have ever truly been alone.

"Thanks. You don't look so bad yourself," I stammer.
"Jamie, thank you again for coming tonight. I know it wasn't where you really wanted to be but I appreciate you being there anyway."

Jamie wraps his arms around my waist and my body comes alive as the warmth of his hands meets my clammy skin. I almost forgot that waiting for me upstairs is the plastic and metal cage that, after tonight, I'll once again return to.

"I would do anything for you or don't you know that by now?"

"I love you Jamie," I whisper.

Jamie smiles and plants a kiss lightly on my cheek and moves to my forehead and down to my neck. His hands begin to make their way from my waist to my neck and then twist around in my hair. My lungs fill up with air almost as quickly as they release it, which is making it really hard to breathe. I curl my fingers through Jamie's hair as his lips part mine. Pins and needles attack my legs and work their way up, moving slowly but increasing every second. I close my eyes and fall into his kiss as he presses his body harder against mine. Is this really happening? Are we about to do what I've been thinking about doing with him from the moment we met?

"Jamie," I say, in between kisses. "Stop."

He pulls back slowly and leans out so he's far enough from my face to allow me to speak without spitting all over him. But his arms remain hard pressed around my back.

"Are you okay?" his voice trembles and his hands fall from me. "Am I moving too fast? Shit, I am aren't I? I swore I'd never be that guy. He slumps against the wall and punches his hands together. It's not funny but a giggle rises from the pit of my stomach. Our roles, for the first time since we started going out, have changed. Tonight, Jamie is the self-conscious one who has the irrational freak-out and I am the one in charge of reassuring *him* that everything is going to be okay.

"It's okay," I say as I slide next to him against the wall. "You weren't going too fast, Jamie."

"I was, ugh God, I am that guy that I hate!"

"Don't be ridiculous. Do you want to know why I said stop?"

Jamie shrugs and nods repeatedly. "Because, and I don't want to jump to any conclusions as to where the night is heading but, I don't want our first time to be in the foyer of my house. I'm pretty sure that my parents walking in on us would kill the moment."

I wrap my arms around his neck and pull him into me. He kisses my forehead and bursts into a fit of laughter at the idea of my parents walking in and seeing their naked daughter and her boyfriend on the floor of the foyer.

"Somehow I think your parents wouldn't like me so much after that," Jamie teases as he slides to his feet. He reaches out his hand for mine and pulls me up. "Seriously, April, we don't have to do this if you're not ready. It's not like I came tonight expecting anything to happen."

I lean in and kiss him for longer than I normally would. His silky lips quiver over mine with every breath and I am not sure I can wait another minute to *truly* be with him.

"Jamie, I love you and if that isn't proof enough that I'm ready for this then let me show you," I whisper.

I take his hand and lead him upstairs and into my bedroom. I take a deep breath and flip on the light as thousands of prying eyes stare down at us. Why did I have to hang so many posters? Now I know what Amber meant when she said I'd never have any privacy in here, not really.

"I think, for the first time ever, I am regretting hanging this many posters on my walls."

"Don't. They may seem intrusive at this moment but don't ever regret what you love," Jamie insists. "I may not be a fan of theirs and I might never truly understand their appeal, but your devotion to them is part of what I love about you."

"So you love the fact that I am also in love with five other men?"

"Hey, like I've said before, guys like a challenge," Jamie teases and kisses me playfully.

We continue to kiss playfully, at first, but then we sink into each other like melting butter. Jamie kisses the base of my neck and makes his way to the edge of my jawbone. He slowly lowers me onto the bed, resting his hand behind my head, and slithers his hands through my hair and across the width of my upper back. Each touch of his finger ignites the pins and needles that had subsided briefly. Our lips meet and part one another as Jamie pushes his body firmly against me. My heart pounds against Jamie's chest as the final piece of my clothing floats to the ground. This is it,

A haze falls over my eyes and everything, except Jamie, fades into the background.

13

My parents go overboard for the Christmas holiday, more twinkling lights then I can count and a blow-up Santa Claus and his reindeer flying off the roof. On the front lawn trees and bushes blink in-sync with some of my dad's favorite Christmas songs. I have trouble falling asleep sometimes and one year our neighbors demanded we tone down our "chaotic display". Of course, Dad being the stubborn man that he is, the decorations never changed.

The interior of the house is no different. A 6-foot tree stands in our living room and every ornament we've ever collected since I was a baby dangles along the sides of the walls. Twinkling lights race through all the rooms, and green wreaths with a large red bow hang off every window and a frighteningly large balloon Santa stands guard in the foyer. My parents dress for the season wearing a red or green article of clothing for 25 days in December and want me to do the same. "I'll wear red socks, even green underwear but I am not wearing a Santa hat to school! "I had to tell them forcefully.

Despite the hiccups I've had so far this year, I'm feeling really festive. It is the first Christmas that I'll have a boyfriend to celebrate with. Jamie is going to spend Christmas Eve with me and Christmas Day with his family and next year we'll switch. I am not sure who is more excited about it, my parents or me. Immediately after I told them the plan they ran out to buy him presents. I have found plenty of gifts for my parents, Grammy and Amber. I, however, cannot find anything suitable for Jamie. This is our first Christmas together and I want it to be special, although I doubt anything will ever be able to top what happened after The Anchor's Halloween party.

With Christmas less than a week away Amber is my last hope. Today she must help me find something for Jamie, something perfect. Jamie is the only reason I have been able to survive this school year and he helped me find strength I never knew I had.

After the incident with the master lock, Jamie has been at my side every day and if someone says something about my brace he'll have some kind of comeback. Last week when Andrew Hijinks shouted, "Hey Robocop don't hurt me!" Jamie put his arm around me and screamed so everyone around heard, "If you don't shut your mouth *she* won't be the one hurting you!" He even came with me to see Dr. Meresh last week when I had a follow up appointment.

Newsflash! The brace isn't coming off anytime soon! "We'll get through this, April," Jamie had said when the disappointing appointment had ended. He has been behind me unconditionally and treating my situation as though it were his own, and I have to find a way to thank him.

"You need to relax April, you're too tense. We're in a mall with tons of stores ripe for the picking. There should be a smile on your face," Amber says as we walk through the sliding doors of The Mall. She is an avid shopper and gets a high from spending money on meaningless items. "Or does Jamie need to give *it* to you again to loosen you up?"

We had to drive almost an hour to Portland where four levels of mall await us with ceilings higher than mall ceilings should be. Twinkling lights, wreaths with giant red bows and miniaturized Christmas trees greet us as we enter the main section of stores. Hordes of people rush by us as they try to find the gifts for their loved ones. I think Amber is the only one who has a smile on her face.

"Shut up, Amber. Don't make me regret telling you," I threaten.

"Okay, okay. So where to?" Amber says, throwing her hands in the air in defeat.

"I don't know where to start," I whine as Amber skips toward Macy's. "I do however, know that I am not going to find anything for Jamie in there."

"You could always give him sex for Christmas. Nothing says Merry Christmas like a good old fashioned banging," Amber twirls like a Ballerina. I curl my lips and furrow my eyebrows as I fold my arms across my chest. I'm too stressed out over what to get for Jamie to deal with her sex jokes. "Ugh, fine. But we're stopping here before we leave," Amber says, pointing at Macy's and blowing a raspberry in my direction.

Not that she ever buys any perfume but she likes walking through the section and taking the free samples that the sales girls hand out.

"How about in here?" I ask pointing to the bright yellow and blue Best Buy sign. "Boys love electronics." Amber's face contorts the way my mom's does when I do something that she considers bad. "What? No good?"

"You love Jamie right? You don't buy the boy you're in love with something from *Best Buy*, April. Trust me on this one. Once I bought ex number three, Christopher Jenkins, a Metallic box set from there and I was all excited to give it to him because it was his favorite band. You remember how many times he made us listen to Ride the Lighting right?"

"At least a hundred times a week," I reply.

"Right, well after I gave him the doomed box set he freaked out. He was convinced that because I had gotten him an 'obvious' gift from the most typical store ever,' I was cheating on him. As you remember, we broke up a few weeks later."

"Seriously? Because of a box set? You said you broke up because he was boring."

"Well, he was but that wasn't why we broke up."

"That is the most ridiculous thing I have ever heard. Jamie would never break up with me over a stupid thing like that."

"Or so you'd think."

I roll my eyes but I walk away from Best Buy anyway.

We swing by a few stores that I toy with the idea of entering but each time Amber pulls me back and gives me some ridiculous reason or another. Over an hour has passed and I haven't found anything that resembles a possible present for Jamie. This is pointless I am never going to find anything. My feet are starting to hurt, my stomach is growling and I'm getting fed up.

"This is useless," I say throwing myself down in defeat on the nearest bench.

"This is your problem, you give up too easily," Amber says swinging her bag of unnecessary new clothing at my legs. "Let's just keep looking."

I don't want to get up. I want to stay here on this bench and wallow in defeat. There is nothing in the whole of the world that is good enough to give to Jamie. Maybe I should cancel the boyfriend aspect of Christmas. It's kind of early to be splitting the holidays anyway, isn't it? Besides, what if he isn't getting me anything? What if I've been freaking out over nothing because he expects that we're not exchanging gifts?

"Look, let's just head back. We've been at this for hours," I suggest.

"Okay Drama Queen we've been here for less than two hours. Now get off your lazy ass and let's go find that boy something spectacular!"

Amber has always been able to say things in such a way that gives me that extra kick in the butt when I need it most. She was the one to get me out of the house when I wanted nothing more than to keep myself locked in my room all year with my brace.

"Ugh, fine but if we don't find anything in the next hour we're leaving. Deal?" I say sticking my hand out.

"You're impossible. Deal," Amber replies shoving her hand in mine for a sealing-the-deal-handshake. "Let's think for a second. What are some of Jamie's likes and dislikes?"

Ha! Like I haven't tried this game before. I will humor her anyway.

"He likes music, all genres. He doesn't like getting lost. He likes watching movies but hates those made-for-TV movies. He doesn't like being labeled by the clothes he wears so he changes his style on a daily basis, which means clothing is out."

"Girl, clothing would be out even if he was the most labeled boy on the planet," Amber giggles. "You need to think bigger than materialistic things."

"Okay, like what?"

"What am I your therapist?" I know she is going to give me examples but since she's Amber she has to screw with me first. It's sort of her thing. Apparently I'm entertaining when I'm squirming. "Ugh, fine if you insist." But I didn't. "Okay so for example: Alex is really into Monster Trucks, like really into them, and I could have easily bought him tickets to some Monster Truck show for his birthday last month. I mean in any world that would be a great gift for someone like him but then I remembered this story he told me about how a few weeks before his dad died, they had gone on this weekend fishing trip. He said that everything about that day was perfect; from the dew on the water to the way the sun rose over the shore like one of those Bob Ross paintings. For hours they sat in a two-person raft with their fishing poles cast into the water waiting for fish to bite and talking about everything. The way Alex spoke about that lake and the boat and that day it clicked for me and although I could never bring his father back I knew exactly what I would get him for his birthday. Next weekend I'm taking him to that same lake in the same tiny boat and we're going to fish using the same rods he and his dad used that day. He practically cried when I told him and everything just kind of came together. That's what I mean by digging deeper. That's what really says, I love you."

I've never heard Amber be so serious before. I mean sure she has her brief moments, like when her aunt died three-years-ago but most of the time she's the least serious person I know. She makes a lot of sense though. Thinking deeper, not focusing on what materialistic gift would be the best thing for him but what would *mean* the most to him. I'm trying to think of the many deep conversations Jamie and I have had but I can't come up with anything.

"Ugh, I can't think of anything meaningful. I suck!" I shout resting my head in my hands and rocking back and forth. "We have had conversations, deep ones. How is it I cannot come up with a single thing that would mean more to him then some stupid CD?"

"Alright I think I know what you need," Amber says pulling me off the bench.

"Peppermint coffee?" I ask dragging behind.

"Peppermint coffee."

Amber and I have this thing; when either of us is really freaking out about something and on the brink of a nervous breakdown we get a cup of peppermint coffee. After a few sips we'd forget whatever it was that was freaking us out and be doubled over with laughter. It is our special thing.

We order our drinks from a nearby coffee cafe and sit on a bench and do what we do best in public places…people watch. An elderly couple breeze by with their hands intertwined. Their faces mirror the years spent together. The man, still blessed with a full head of silver hair, kisses his wife gently as they continue on their day of shopping. It's a simple gesture but it's obvious that they're still in love. I wonder if Jamie and I will be together till we're the ones with silver hair, old and wrinkled but still pleased to have one another's company. "Do you think you can love only one person for the rest of your life?" I ask Amber.

Amber nearly chokes on her coffee. I didn't plan on asking her because I didn't realize I was thinking it.

"Was that a rhetorical question or do you really want my opinion?"

I'm not really sure; part of me is dying to know what Amber thinks. She always seems to have an answer for everything that deals with matters of the heart and when she isn't sure she makes something up that is so brilliant it might as well be true.

"I really want to know. Do you think you can love the same person for your entire life? Without wavering or being unfaithful? I say without looking up from my coffee cup. I can't look her in the eye I'm so embarrassed at how pathetic I am for asking.

"I think anything is possible so I do think that people can stay in love, like googly-eyes, unable to keep their hands off one another, romance movie kind of love. I think it is incredibly rare but I think it can happen,"

Amber is as serious as she can be but there's something in her inflection that makes me nervous. Maybe she doesn't think Jamie and I are one of those couples who can last a lifetime? Maybe she knows something I don't? Maybe she thinks that I am an idiot for even thinking that it is possible to love Jamie for the rest of my life? I have half a mind to ask her but the other half is too afraid to speak. Besides, Amber isn't a fortuneteller so how could she know that Jamie and I won't last? Her opinion matters but it isn't the end all be all of, well, anything. I need to focus on the task at hand. I need to figure out what to get Jamie for our first Christmas together. I can worry about our forever later.

"Okay ," Amber says, "so I'm in my room last night watching some stupid reality show and mom comes charging in like a bull and starts ranting about how irresponsible I am because I haven't applied to every college in the United States yet."

Ever since Ms. Eleanor, Amber's guidance counselor, told the Hills that their daughter had the grades to get into an Ivy League school Mrs. Hill has been college crazy. They ordered catalogues from Harvard, Princeton, Yale, Brown, Columbia and Dartmouth and have been forcing Amber to review one catalogue a night for the last week. She has options but Amber still doesn't know what she wants to do with her life so college is not in the forefront of her mind yet.

I know what I want to do with my life but most of the schools with the best creative writing programs are in New York and California and I'm not sure I want to move that far away. "Nope and I refuse to until I figure out what the hell I'm going to do with the rest of my life," Amber insists. "I will not be one of those girls who goes to a college because their parents want them to. I am going to be rich and successful, doing what well that remains to be seen."

Amber is the type of person that could probably succeed at any career she wants to have definitely something that requires a lot of talking and negotiation.

But I still need to get a present for Jamie.

"So I'm thinking we take one last swing around the second floor and then give up."

Amber sighs, but follows and we head for the escalators with our peppermint coffees in tow.

The second floor holds most of the apparel stores so naturally it is the most crowded. Amber and I push our way through a sea of people.

"Ugh this is ridiculous!" Amber says as she pushes her way through, somehow ignoring the dozens of bodies plowing into us.

Because I am wearing my brace I am having trouble being jostled by the crowd. We make our way slowly and I can see the windows and entrances to the shops. Each one is decorated for the holidays. Miniature Christmas trees light up the corners of the store windows and illuminate the manikins. We have already passed half of the stores on the second floor, my last floor of hope, when something grabs my attention.

In a snowflake sprinkled window a manikin stands on a mountain of presents. It's not the heap of presents that catches my eye it's a leather jacket with Army patch embroidery on the chest pockets that has my heart fluttering. I remember a conversation Jamie and I had about his Grandfather, James (his namesake), who was a World War II veteran. "My Grandfather was everything to me. I love my parents but I always felt more connected to my Grandfather," Jamie had said. "I also looked forward to his visits because he would tell me old war stories and then take me out for a guy's night or for an aimless drive around so we could spend time just the two of us." Jamie also told me about the jacket that Grandpa James always wore. "He had this old leather Army jacket, which was a gift from my Grandma Eileen, who died when I was just a baby. The jacket was brown leather and had green Army patches embroidered into the chest. It didn't matter the temperature outside, Grandpa wore that jacket in the middle of the summer heat. He believed it was his last link to Eileen and wearing it kept him close to her."

"Where is the jacket now," I asked.

"Unfortunately Grandpa died a-year-ago and even though he contemplated giving me the jacket he couldn't part with it so he was buried with that jacket."

Although he understood, I knew Jamie was devastated because that jacket was his last remaining link to his Grandpa and now displayed in front of me is *that jacket*. Sure, it's not worn out and fraying at the shoulders like Grandpa James' was but it is the exact same jacket, I am sure of it. Jamie showed me a picture of it and this is it!

"Oh my God!" I shout stopping Amber mid step, "This is it!"

"Geez you nearly gave me a heart attack. What's it?" Amber says looking through the store window.

"This, the jacket," I tap on the glass to direct Amber's eyes to the right place. "This is exactly what I was looking for."

Amber's eyes twinkle and she grabs my hand and drags me into the store. I am feeling exhilarated and am already picturing Jamie's reaction when I give him the jacket. I wonder if he'll cry. No, I hope he doesn't. I would feel terrible if I made him cry. As I pull the jacket off the hanger I feel overwhelmed with emotion myself. I feel like with this jacket I can give Jamie a piece of his Grandfather back and I can't think of anything better than that.

14

It's Christmas Eve, my first with Jamie, and I have absolutely nothing festive to wear. How is this possible? Every other year I've worn something either red or green topped off with this cute Santa hat that sings *Jingle Bells* every time I rock my head back and forth. This year all of my red and green outfits seem really ugly and the Santa hat is just stupid. Besides everything I have tried on with this brace makes me look like I am this year's Christmas tree, which is so fitting considering it is the opposite of how I want to look around Jamie.

He's seen the entire brace and yet I am still freaking out about what to wear around him. I thought the whole insecure thing went away after the first few weeks of a relationship especially after the couple has had sex; shouldn't I be able to walk around him in my pajamas by now or at the very least sweats? Screw it! I am just going to pick out the first festive dress I find that can fit over the brace and that is going to be that.

I slide into the red quarter sleeve dress with the bedazzled snowflake on the chest and it barely fits but it will have to do because I refuse to throw another outfit into the "my brace tore a hole in the fabric," pile on my bed. I grab one of the black hair ties off the dresser and tie my hair into a ponytail and complete it with a red and green headband. I'm not about to wear the Santa hat but if I don't wear some kind of Christmas headdress my parents will give me grief about it all night. One quick glance in the mirror and I am as good as I am going to get in the two minutes before Jamie is scheduled to arrive. I pull out the wrapped box where the jacket is hidden beneath two layers of sparkle wrapping paper and silver bow. I feel giddy thinking about giving it to him.

Ding dong! That must be Jamie! I can't believe my first boyfriend Christmas is about to begin! Eek!

I hear one of my parents shuffle to the front door. "Hi Jamie," my father says. "Merry Christmas-Eve!"

"Merry Christmas Eve to you too Mr. Marks," Jamie replies.

"Oh come on Jamie, you can be calling me Jason by now," my father insists.

As they're engaged in polite chatter, I make one last check on the wrapping job, take a swift glance in the mirror and head downstairs.

My parents have Jamie huddled by the fire. He must be sweltering with all the heat from the fire and the thickness of his sweater. When I invited him to join us for Christmas Eve I had warned him about my parent's obsession with the holiday and joked that he would have to wear something festive, I didn't think he would actually do it. I feel like I am looking at a scene from a caveman movie as I approach the three most important people in the world to me. They're all sitting close together with their legs and arms folded. My parents have shut off all the downstairs lights leaving only the flickering fire and twinkling lights to illuminate the house.

"So Jamie, now that we know each other a bit, tell me, what are your intentions with our daughter?" my father teases.

Jamie unfolds his arms and looks like a truck hit him. I know when my dad is joking but my poor caught-off-guard boyfriend does not.

"Wha...what?" Jamie stutters.

I can almost see the sweat beading on his forehead.

"What do you intend on doing with her? Are you with her for the long haul or are you just in it for the nookie?" my father says raising his voice.

"Nookie? No, Sir I…" Jamie stammers.

"Just know that if you break her heart I will come down on you so hard you'll wish…"

"Dad, stop that!" I say as I enter the living room. Of course, in my mind I am picturing myself swooping in like a superhero there to save Jamie from the big bad dad. "He doesn't know you well enough to know when you're teasing. It's just mean."

Jamie bolts to his feet and can't get to me fast enough. He wraps his arms around me but it's more than a hug it's like a giant "thank you." I wonder what else my father, or my mother for that matter, said before I came downstairs. I shoot my parents a warning look.

"I swear I was good," my mom says raising her arms in the air like she's being arrested.

"Dad?" I say, taking the same tone he uses on me when he knows I'm guilty of something.

"I could have been worse. Come on honey you know we had to break him in. If he's going to roll with *my* kid he has to be able to handle your crazy parents," Dad retorts.

Jamie pulls away and winks. "You're right Jason, that look on her face is priceless."

Now I'm confused. "What is going on?"

"Sorry kiddo I couldn't resist," my dad says as he high fives Jamie.

They're messing with me. My parents knew I was nervous about tonight and they wanted to get a good laugh at my expense. I'm glad to see Jamie and my parents get along so well but I wish they would get along about something that doesn't nearly give me a heart attack.

"Ha-freaking-ha. Very funny," I say in the most monotone voice I can possibly make. "Let's make April jump out of her skin for the holidays. Yay."

Jamie lifts me in a twirling hug and kisses me gently on the cheek. Okay, fine I forgive him but I'm still mad at my parents, especially my dad.

"So, is that my gift?" Jamie asks pointing to the present that I'm still clinging to.

I jerk it behind my back as if that will prevent him from thinking about it.

"I forgot I was holding it," I respond. "I meant to slip it under the tree before you saw it."

"Well then," Jamie says quietly and moves aside and bows as I walk by.

I place the present under the tree, which has so many red and green wrapped gifts there isn't much room for anything else. I wonder which gift is from Jamie. Every size gift imaginable is under this tree; did he get me jewelry? Charlie used to get me jewelry all the time, nothing too spectacular, but always something different. Half of my jewelry collection came from him. Amber always said I was lucky that Charlie doted on me like that but it always felt like bribery to me. Sort of, "If you remain my girlfriend I'll keep buying you jewelry."

"Well, Jamie, since you're new to our Christmas traditions we will ease you in gently," my mom says gleefully.

In this house around the holidays I'm not really sure what "gently" means. I can't imagine my parents being willing to change up our holiday traditions just because Jamie is here. Every year while mom cooks dinner, usually a goose or some kind of pasta dish, dad and I sit in the living room reading, *Twas the Night Before Christmas*. Once dinner is ready we gather around the table and have a festive meal. Once dinner is done we go into the living room for hot chocolate, Christmas tree shaped sugar cookies and to sing Christmas carols. Some years, if the weather allows, we go caroling around our neighborhood. Once the caroling is complete, meaning after we've visited the Martins and they've told us to get off their stoop, we go home to open presents. This is our holiday tradition and it never changes. Crap! I wish I had remembered the caroling and singing before I invited Jamie over. I sound like a dying cat when I sing.

"So no caroling this year?" I ask, crossing my fingers behind my back.

"Oh no, of course we're caroling this year," mom replies. "It wouldn't be Christmas without the Martins yelling at us."

"Really? But mom," I start but am swiftly interrupted by an overzealous boyfriend.

"You go caroling?" Jamie jumps in and is practically beaming.

"Yeah," I say under my breath.

"Girl can hold a tune I tell ya," my father says as he brushes by and places a hand on Jamie's shoulder.

"Can she now?" Jamie says looking at me like I'm some world famous musician. "Alright Ms. April let's hear those chops."

"No way! Absolutely not."

"She's just shy right now. You just wait until we go a-caroling Mr. Clarke you are going to be impressed with our girl here, "dad exclaims.

"Well then, what are we waiting for? Let's get our caroling on!" Jamie boasts.

"Okay first of all the fact that you're excited about hearing me sing proves just how unprepared you are for a Marks' Christmas," I tease. "Secondly we don't go caroling until after dessert. Trust me my singing is truly nothing to boast about."

"Oh come on April, don't pretend like you weren't looking forward to tonight. If I'm not mistaken I saw you change your outfit at least five times before Jamie got here," my dad says as my mother shakes her head to try to get him to stop but it's too late.

I don't want to sing in front of him because contrary to my father's delusions I can't carry a tune even if I wanted to. I've heard Jamie sing before and if anyone can carry a tune it's him, which makes the idea of singing in front of him more terrifying and mortifying.

"Mom, dad, can I talk to you for a minute?" I ask before my mom heads off to the kitchen to finish cooking dinner.

"Sure, what's up?" dad asks as he throws himself on the couch with *'Twas the Night Before Christmas*.

"In private please," I say motioning for them to follow me into the foyer. They do.

"Sweetie what is this about? You're being rude to your guest," mom says sternly.

"I know but this will just take a second," I promise. "Look you know how much I love our holiday traditions and not once have I asked to skip out on any of our festivities, right?" Both my parents nod in agreement. "I just thought that since it is Jamie's first Christmas with us, and it's my first Christmas with him, that maybe we could skip out on the caroling and spend some time together...just the two of us. I have a present that I'd really like to give him, in private."

Once the words leave my mouth I hear how incriminating they sound and apparently so does my father. His face contorts, his eyes are wide, his mouth dropped and his cheeks turn as red as my dress. To them it must sound like I am planning on giving Jamie my virginity for Christmas. I haven't told my parents about what happened after the Halloween party and I don't think I ever will. I don't want them to stop letting Jamie come over or worse, lecture me about the birds and the bees. Brilliant choice of words April. I need to mend this situation and quickly otherwise it's *We Wish You a Merry Christmas* for me.

"No, that's not what I meant," I stammer trying to rectify the situation. "I just meant that, I spent hours at the stupid Mall looking for the perfect gift for him and just when I was about to give up there it was staring at me. It's the perfect gift and I want to give it to him in private. You know I'd never ask if it weren't important to me. Come on of all people you two should understand how I am feeling. I highly doubt you would have wanted to spend your first Christmas together with Grandma and Grandpa."

My parents exchange sinister glances and burst into a wild giggle. I'm not sure what I've said that is so funny but I don't really like being laughed at.

"She's babbling, Jason," mom says to my father in between giggles.

"It must be important then," dad replies matching my mother's immature laughter.

"Excuse me?" I chime in and cross my arms.

"We always know when something is important to you because you start babbling about it," mom says catching her breath and allowing the giggle to recede. "When you were five you wanted this rocking horse so badly you went on for almost half an hour about it. Eventually we bought it just to shut you up."

"You're comparing my boyfriend to a freaking rocking horse?"

"I guess so, but please don't take my comparison literally when you're alone with him later and are giving him your special present," my mother says with a wink.

"Gross! Mom, stop that. You know that isn't what I meant!"

"Yeah, Anna, please stop," my dad, says with disgust. "Joking about my daughter having sex isn't Christmassy."

I just want this conversation to end, whatever the outcome.

"So?" I ask.

"It's fine with me if it's okay with your father," mom says plainly.

I turn to my father and cup my hands together pleadingly.

"Okay, but you keep your light on, door and blinds open at all times," dad says using his finger for emphasis. "And remember a father always knows what is going on even when he isn't in the room."

I roll my eyes. I appreciate him trying to be threatening but staring at me with his bifocals it's really hard to take his threats seriously. Jamie towers over my dad and his arms are about the size of dad's neck; somehow I don't see him being intimidated by this middle-aged man either.

"I promise," I reply putting two fingers up like I'm still in girl scouts. "Scout's honor."

My parents exchange a few silent words communicating through their minds, something they do far too often. I think my parents can actually read minds. Either that or they're aliens.

"Okay," my father says once their mental communication has ended, "I suppose you can skip caroling this year."

I let out a squeal and wrap my parents in a group hug and sprint back into the living room for holiday tradition number one.

I am really looking forward to reading *'Twas.* In fact, every tradition this year is thrilling because they're all just one-step closer to the moment when I can have Jamie all to myself and I can finally give him his present. I just hope Jamie wasn't really looking forward to caroling.

15

Jamie is getting along famously with my parents and I'm really in the whole Christmas spirit. However, I wouldn't mind if dessert would go a little faster considering I can hardly sit still. I don't pay much attention to the conversation during dinner except when my name is mentioned. Of course my ears perk up for these stories because I have to make sure my parents don't tell Jamie anything too incriminating. Luckily I've trained them well and they steer clear of any April pooping stories and stick to cutesy tales of how adorable and creative and loving I was and still am.

Finally it's time for the parental units to go caroling and for us to have our alone time. Jamie excuses himself from the living room, where my parents prepare their voices, I grab the gift from under the tree and sprint it upstairs to my bedroom. I come down in time to see Jamie waving my parents off on their caroling adventure. He shuts the front door and turns to face me with his hands snug inside the pockets of his slacks. He is so damn handsome. Standing here with Jamie's arms wrapped around my waist, or what should be my waist but is actually the plastic part of the brace (yuck), the idea of sex does seem appealing. But I promised my father I wouldn't, although internally I just promising not to do it tonight. I just wish Jamie would stop looking at me like that. With the twinkle in his eyes and his crooked smile, it's killing me.

"So where's this perfect gift you told your parents about?' Jamie asks and squeezes the small of my back pulling me into him.

"Crap! You heard all that?" I ask.

"The foyer isn't exactly soundproof, April."

I smack my hand to my forehead. "I sounded like a five-year-old."

Jamie pulls my hand off my forehead and kisses it. "I think it happens to be adorable that you wanted me all to yourself tonight and if I'm being honest I've wanted to get you all to myself all night."

I give him a peck on the lips but now my heart is racing and my head is foggy. Does he want me alone because he expects sex? Maybe going upstairs isn't the best idea. If we do I don't think I'll be able to resist and God forbid my parents hit the Martins house first and come home early and catch us. The thought makes me shiver.

"Cold?" Jamie asks as he rapidly rubs my arms producing heat.

Cold is the last thing I am feeling right now. Oh how I wish I were wearing black right now then maybe the sweat stains would be less obvious. Damn my parents and their silly Christmas festive traditions.

"I'm okay," I say stepping out of his arms. "Why don't you wait here and I'll get your gift and bring it down to you."

"I thought you wanted to give it to me in your room?"

"I did but it's actually not an in-my-room kind of a gift," I am babbling again.

Jamie smiles, another irresistible smirk. "April, if you don't want me in your room because you didn't clean up just let me know. But if you don't want me coming up because you think I'm expecting something to happen then you needn't worry. I don't think we're going to have sex now every time we're alone. Besides, as your father said, sex isn't very Christmassy."

I feel like the Wicked Witch of the West because I am basically melting on the stairs right now.

"Why do you have to be so damn perfect, Jamie?"

"It's a gift," Jamie says matter-of-factly.

"Well, well someone is cocky tonight."

"Not tonight, remember?" Jamie says and winks.

I slap his arm and shove him lightly. "I love you, Jamie."

"I love you too, April."

I take his hand and lead him upstairs where the only undressing Jamie will be doing will be of the wrapping paper.

16

Every time Jamie is in my room it looks smaller, but not in the walls-closing-in kind of way. It's the intimate; wish it could be smaller, kind of feeling. I remember the first time he was in my room when I finally had the guts to tell him about my obsession with the Backstreet Boys. I figured he handled the whole my girlfriend could pass for a robot thing perfectly; he must be ready for my crazier quality. He was obviously overwhelmed by all of the posters but he never made fun of me. He doesn't like their music but he also doesn't fault me for liking them the way Charlie used to or the way Amber sometimes does. At first I was embarrassed about all the eyes gawking at us but now none of it bothers me. Jamie plops on the desk chair and spins around placing his hands behind his head.

"So how's your book coming along?" Jamie asks.

"Surprisingly well actually," I reply gleefully. "I think once I am done with the next two chapters I'll be ready for my first round of editing."

Ever since I found the jacket something has opened in me and my muse has been holding on tight. I have been writing vigorously whenever I get the chance and if I'm not near a computer I'll jot a few notes down on a receipt or gum wrapper, or whatever else I can find in my purse.

When I am home I spend two to three hours writing but I've been able to write nearly the entire manuscript with the exception of the last two chapters. It's nowhere near ready to be submitted and there's no way I'm letting anyone read it yet but hey, at least I'm writing.

"See, I knew you had it in you," Jamie says leaping off the chair and wrapping his arms around my waist.

"Yeah, well you've inspired me."

Kissing him is like flying. I'm so lost in his touch that I have almost forgotten about the present.

"So, this gift of yours, how important is it that you give it to me first?" Jamie asks, as he pulls back but keeps his arms around my waist.

"No. I mean, I guess not. Why?" I reply.

"Well," he says pulling a small box out from the front pockets of his trousers. "I have something I have been dying to give you all night."

The box is a petite black velvet ring box with a golden trim. I'm feeling equal parts excitement and fear that he is about to propose. Is he really about to pull out an engagement ring? Why isn't he on one knee? Is he going to give me a long speech and then drop? As much as I love him and know we are going to spend the rest of our lives together if we got engaged now my parents, laid back as they are, would flip out. And I can hear Amber's comments now, "You are a hopeless romantic," and "Come back to the real world, April. Marriage only has a 50/50 chance of lasting." She's not cynical nor does she think all marriage ends in divorce but she, like everyone else, believes that people who get married before they're at least 25-years-old will likely end up divorced within a year. People like her sister, Mary.

Mary married her high school sweetheart, Albert, right after graduation. After a few years of marriage Albert left her for another woman and Mary was forced to move back home for a while until she moved out to Los Angeles. Things at home became stressful for Amber and her family and I think since then she's had a hard time believing that young marriages have any hope of lasting.

I want to push pause on this moment so I can run like the Flash and open the box and see what's inside. If he asks I'll say yes because there is no one else in the world I would rather spend my life with than Jamie Still, I feel the sweat on my neck as Jamie walks toward me with the box settled in the palm of his hand. I picture all of the ways the rest of tonight can go after this and all of the screaming that is going to take place when I tell my parents that I'm engaged. But I'm not afraid. In fact, I know that this is right that everything in my life has been leading me to this moment. This is what is supposed to happen so screw all the doubters and naysayers!

"I thought long and hard about what to get you. Something I knew you would truly like. It had to be something with meaning. I looked for weeks but nothing was ever good enough and then I found the perfect gift. It was something I knew you would love and it would also prove to you that despite what has been said about men, some of us do actually listen," Jamie explains and begins to peel back the lid of the box.

I see something folded inside which he lifts out and hands to me. Only when it's in my hand do I realize what it is, a Concert ticket! But not just a regular concert ticket, an impossible-to-get front row ticket to *The Backstreet Boys* concert at the Portland Arena for this summer! Tickets that sold out nearly 30 seconds after they went on sale! It is the first time the boys will be in the Maine area in years. I slide the ticket through my fingers and realize there are actually two tickets here. This time I hope I am not wrong about what it means.

"Just in case you're wondering the second ticket is for me," Jamie says and digs in his pockets. "That is, if you want me there."

I wrap my arms around his neck and swing myself into his arms. I kiss him on the lips and then plant smaller but forceful ones on the rest of his face and neck. He is laughing at every one of them. He really did listen to me. After we had been dating for a while Jamie asked me about my Backstreet Boys obsession and I had explained that I found their music at a time when I needed them most, shortly after my Grandmother passed away. They were my saving grace and the only reason I was able to get past her death. Later when I was diagnosed with scoliosis they were the only things that kept me from falling into a depression. I believe that they have saved me and Jamie seemed to understand it too. I had told him about the concert in Portland and how depressed I was about not being able to get tickets to their show. Actually I know I said, "I would give anything to go to that concert." Still, he heard me. He knew exactly what these tickets would mean to me and it truly meant everything.

"April," Jamie says pushing my shoulders in an attempt to get me to stop kissing him. "As much as I love feeling your lips all over me I do have one more thing to give to you."
There's more? How could there be more?

With angels singing in the background, (okay maybe not real angels but in my head I hear them), Jamie pulls two laminated white and blue badges out of his pocket. He doesn't have to finish unveiling them for me to know what they are. I squeal with delight and nearly knock us both over as I lunge into him, and I'm kissing him so hard that we along with the badges with the red lettering

reading, *All Access,* fall to the ground. I relent on the kissing fiasco

and straddle him so he can't move.

"How did you get these?" I scream.

"I have my ways," Jamie replies vaguely. He smirks and I

know there is more to the story.

"Seriously, Jamie, how did you get the tickets let alone the

passes?"

"I am super cool."

"NO! I *don't* think you're super cool!"

Jamie quickly turns on his side and I topple over onto my

back beside him. We're both laughing hysterically.

"Fine. You really want to know?" Jamie asks resting his head

on his arm. I nod. "Okay you remember a few weeks ago when I said

I was going to visit my Aunt Lucy in the hospital because she

slipped and fell on dog shit?"

"Yes. How is she by the way?"

Jamie lets out a wicked laugh and I realize the whole story

was a ruse. I should have known.

"Well, there was no dog shit. I was actually in Portland at the Portland Arena Box Office standing in line with hundreds of teenage girls and their mothers, all whom would not stop singing *Backstreet Boys* songs, waiting for the tickets to go on sale. Now I am not exaggerating when I say that I was the only person there with a penis. It took me a few rounds of testosterone to feel like a man again but I did make friends with this lovely sixty-year-old woman and her thirteen-year-old Granddaughter. Turns out they were there because the Grandmother was a fan of the boys and wanted to show her Granddaughter who they were," Jamie explains. "Anyway I waited with practically every girl in Portland on that line from 4 o'clock in the morning until 10 o'clock a.m. when the tickets went on sale. But they sold out before I even got up to the box office door!

"Like everyone else snubbed by your wonderful boys and their ridiculously quick sell out, I could have just gone home and given up. However, luckily for you, your boyfriend is *not* like every other teenage girl and their mother in Portland. I waited until the crowd cleared out and marched up to the box office and demanded to speak with the manager. Michael, the manager, agreed to speak with me and we had a long chat and after a lot of soul searching, Michael told me to grow up and go home. But when your face popped into my head I realized that there was no way I could go home without those tickets. So I marched back into Michael's office and told him I was not going to leave until he got someone on the phone that *could* get me the tickets. An hour later I had in my possession two front row tickets and two all access passes."

Jamie finishes his story with a wide and suspicious grin; there is no way this Michael guy gave him front row tickets and all access passes because he begged the guy into submission.

"Oh my God, Jamie Clarke, you bribed him didn't you?" I whisper, because clearly bribery warrants whispering. Jamie winks and jumps to his feet but neither confirms nor denies my accusation. I know the truth. "Ha, ha! Jamie Clarke you little sneak, you really bribed the manager of the Portland Arena for me?"

"You'll never get me to confess," Jamie says pulling me to my feet and wrapping his arms around the small of my back, the only space the brace isn't covering. "Now, will you give me my present already? I'm dying over here."

I almost forgot about his present. I shuffle to the bed where I flung the present right before I attacked Jamie and learned that, despite his insistence that he would never use his family's money to get ahead in life, he had used his wealth to get me the ultimate gift. Well, the ultimate gift for a Backstreet Boys fan that is.

"Like you," I start, "I did a lot of searching and panicking over what to get you. I had no clue what you might want or need since you have a tendency to not like to share in that way."

"I am mysterious in that way, aren't I?" Jamie brags.

"*Anyway*. Even though you gave me nothing to go on, I didn't have to bribe anyone to get this for you. I remembered that story you told me about that jacket your Grandfather had and how important it was to you and well…here," I say handing him the present.

My insides churn and everything seems to be moving in slow motion. He rips the wrapping paper slowly. I want him to hurry up and just rip the thing open already the anticipation is killing me. I have never been one for taking my time. Even when I was younger and I would eat those Tootsie pops I always bit right into them so I could get to the center as quickly as possible. I hold the record in my family for the fastest present opener and can shred through three gifts in under a minute. My parents always used to tease me about how proud I made them as if it were some great skillset or something. I guess I could always become one of the girls who sit in an elf costume wrapping presents at the mall for $9.50 an hour during the holidays. Clearly Jamie is not cut out for such a career. Finally he slides the jacket out of the box and his face goes white, stark white like he's seen a ghost. He claps his hand over his mouth and tears begin to well in his eyes.

"Jamie?" I ask gently. He's so silent and so still I'm not even sure he's breathing. I can't tell if he's happy with the gift or if I've overstepped my boundaries as his girlfriend. "Did I? I mean, is this okay?"

He won't look at me or at anything except for the jacket. I have a million thoughts racing through my mind like maybe I should have stuck with the material things like a CD or a gift card. Maybe I was being too optimistic in thinking I was giving him something truly meaningful with this jacket. Maybe the memory of the jacket and his Grandfather is still too painful and all I've done with my gift is raise those feelings of loss and trauma over losing Grandpa James. This silence is killing me. I go over to my bed and sit on the edge of it facing Jamie. My legs won't stop shaking and my hands remain clammy no matter how many times I wipe them on my dress. I prefer the nervousness I was feeling earlier to the nerves running through me right now. Why can't I be that girlfriend who after a few weeks just slides into the relationship like she would a pair of jeans? Why do I have to over-analyze everything? Why do I have to let my fears and insecurities get the best of me, especially when it comes to Jamie? He has proven time and time again that he is in this relationship 100% and yet I can't seem to shake the sinking feeling that something is going to go wrong. That somehow I am going to end up losing him.

"Jamie?" I try again. "Are you angry with me?"

Folding the jacket and placing it under his arm he places himself beside me on the bed. He takes my hand and places it in his lap. With his thumb he rubs the space between my ring and middle fingers and half smiles. His legs tremble and his hands, although not clammy, are hot and I can feel how rapid his pulse is.

"April, this gift…" Jamie starts but his voice trails off and cracks. "Thank you."

He leans in and kisses me softly on the forehead but keeps my hands contained within his. His face flushes and his eyes are watery. "You like it?" I ask shyly.

"Are you kidding me," Jamie replies as his lips part and turn up into a wide grin. "I love it. I mean it is exactly like the one my Grandfather had. I didn't think I would ever see this jacket again. Thank you so much, April, you really are everything to me."

17

"April, we're home!" my father calls from downstairs.

My parents have always had the worst timing in the world. Somehow they always know just when to interrupt something that I don't want interrupted.

"Looks like they went to the Martin's a little early this year," I say. I jump off the bed and store the tickets and passes in my desk drawer for safekeeping.

Jamie slides off the bed and wraps the jacket around his shoulders. He looks so handsome in it; I start for the door but notice that Jamie isn't following me.

"You coming?" I ask as I turn to face him.

"April," Jamie says, as his voice takes a tone I've never heard. It's low and serious. "When I pulled out the box with your tickets, did you think I was going to propose?"

I don't know what to say. Maybe if I stand perfectly still and remain quiet he'll forget about it. It's mortifying to think your boyfriend of only a few months is going to propose only to find out that you were completely delusional, as usual. I really don't want to answer him. But instead...

"No, of course not," I lie.

"Oh okay," Jamie says and I swear I hear a hint of disappointment. "That's good, I guess."

"Jamie?" I ask. "What is it?"

"Nothing. I thought maybe you thought there was an engagement ring in the box and I didn't want you to get the wrong idea." He was stammering, "Umm we'd better get downstairs we wouldn't want your parents thinking something was going on up here. I'd hate to get on their bad side."

Like that could ever happen. We head downstairs in silence with this awkward elephant between us.

Jamie can hardly look at me and I want to rewind that moment Jamie asked me about the box and I want to suck it up and tell him the truth. I'll pull him aside before he leaves and explain to him why I lied and that I did think he was going to propose. The worst he can do is say that he isn't ready for that step and that is okay because I'm not either. Sometimes I am too insecure for my own good. If I could wake up a different person tomorrow I would and I'd make sure I was someone who didn't always second-guess herself.

"So, tell us," my mother starts, "what he give you?"

"Wha...what? Nothing!" I shout, because clearly my mother is asking if Jamie and I had sex while they were gone.

"For Christmas. I assume you guys exchanged gifts already," mom clarifies.

"Oh, right. Of course, I knew that," I stammer.

"Sure you did," my father says flatly.

I look at Jamie and smile but he gives me a half smile in return. I want to be excited about the tickets and the passes but seeing the broken look on my boyfriend's face it is hard to be excited about anything. I have to fix this.

"Jamie, can I speak with you for a minute?" I ask and begin to head for the foyer. Jamie nods and heads out of the room behind me. "We'll be right back," I say to my parents.

"Is everything okay?" mom asks.

I shrug and head into the foyer to speak with Jamie.

"Hey, you okay?" I ask, as I tug at the sleeve on his shirt.

"I'm fine," he replies flatly. "But we're being rude to your parents so we should probably head back in."

He starts for the living room but I grab his wrist and tug at him until he stops. "Jamie, please talk to me. You're obviously angry with me for something and I deserve to know why"

"It's nothing. I'm not mad," Jamie sighs and faces me. "If you want the truth, I'm hurt."

"Hurt? Why?"

"Look, I know we've only been together for a few months but I thought we were on the same page, you know with you being everything to me and all."

"We are."

"Then why did you lie to me before about what you thought was inside the box?"

I shouldn't be shocked that Jamie knew I was lying, he knows me really well.

"I'm sorry I lied," I say. My voice is muffled as I bury my face in my hands. "I was embarrassed and honestly a little afraid."

I'm still hiding but Jamie slides beside me and pulls my forearms forward to remove my hands from my face. When I look at him he's giving me a crooked smile.

"Were you afraid when you thought it was an engagement ring?" Jamie asks and wraps his arm around my shoulders and pulls me into him.

"I don't want to say," I reply nervously.

"April, please tell me. Were you afraid?"

I sigh and count to ten, as my mother always tells me to do when I feel like I'm going to panic. I'm afraid I am going to scare him away. Amber always says that boys our age are terrified of the idea of marriage. The whole concept of us being in love should comfort me but being in love and discussing marriage are two very different things. Fingers crossed he doesn't run away so fast he leaves a Jamie-shaped hole in the front door.

"No, I wasn't afraid," I whisper and try to keep the shakiness in my voice at a minimum. "Actually, I was excited. I mean I was a little surprised and a little nervous about what my parents would say but the idea of committing myself to you for the rest of my life wasn't scary at all."

Well, I went for it and I went all in. Now there's nothing left to do but wait for the gavel to come down.

"Can I be honest with you?" Jamie asks, "I've thought about proposing to you, getting down on one knee and promising to love you for the rest of our lives if you'd have me. I've probably thought about it more times than a boy my age should and I don't know if that makes me any less of a man but if it does then it's a sacrifice I'm willing to make."

My heart is beating so hard it might as well just leap out of my chest and plant itself on Jamie. The words coming out of his mouth say everything I have ever wanted to hear from him. I feel like we're unbreakable and this is where we're meant to be...together.

"If you've been feeling this way, why you haven't you proposed?"

Jamie let's out a wild laugh. "April, we're in high school! We would need our parents' permission to get married and I know for a fact mine wouldn't give it and somehow, despite how cool they are, I doubt your parents would either. Besides I think marrying you would probably make more sense when we both have jobs and can afford a place of our own. I don't think living in our parents' basement would be ideal housing."

God, I love the way he speaks sometimes. It's like he's an old soul placed inside a teenage boy's body.

"Good point. Plus when we're married I'd rather not have my mommy still doing my laundry."

We both laugh, neither one of us want to be that ridiculous married couple who is still living with their parents.

"But just know, when we're old enough and can fend for ourselves the first thing I am doing is going out and buying you that ring."

"You know, I love you, Jamie."

"And you know I love you too, April."

I never thought I would find everything I ever wanted while I was still in high school, especially not after my last visit to Dr. Meresh. Now my future is set! No matter what happens from now on, no matter what college I attend or what career path I decide to go on, Jamie will be by my side and that's all I really need to know.

18

Jamie has asked me to go with him to Boston during our semester break and visit his Grandpa James' memorial on the anniversary of his death. He wants to "introduce" me to his grandfather. "Okay, that's kind of weird," Amber had said when I told her about the trip and why Jamie wanted me to come along.

Amber doesn't believe in the afterlife. To her the idea of spirits hanging around their loved ones is preposterous. She thinks you live, you die and that's it. Jamie doesn't believe that everyone turns into ghosts when they die but he has said that when he visits his Grandfather's grave he feels like Grandpa James can hear him. Me? I'm not sure what I believe. It would be comforting to believe that our loved ones' spirits hang around long after their bodies are gone so they can look out for those they've left behind. I think it would make the concept of death a little easier but when Grandma Maggie died I never felt her around; she was just gone.

Since it's only an hour and a half from Perkins Harbor and we wouldn't need to stay over, my parents agreed to let me go. They're big Jamie fans but the idea of letting their teenage daughter stay overnight with her boyfriend in another city – NO. I have been to Boston a few times and although I am in no way a Red Sox fan, I love the city. It is so different from Perkins Harbor with its massive buildings, traffic, and crowded streets and of course, Fenway Park. I've never seen the inside of the ballpark because my dad says the Red Sox's fans can get really rowdy and he doesn't want to expose me to that kind of chaos just yet. I think it would be really exciting to see the stadium erupted during a game, especially against their rivals the New York Yankees. Here in Perkins we don't have a lot of car traffic, it's mostly pedestrian but in Boston there always seems to be some kind of event going on whether it is a farmer's market, street fair or sports game, the city is always buzzing. The first time I was there was almost like a culture shock for me. But Jamie grew up in Boston so for him it is like going home.

"If we have time maybe I can show you where I grew up," Jamie says as we pull off the interstate entering into Boston.

"I'd love that," I reply and squeeze Jamie's hand, which I have been holding the entire trip.

I know today is going to be difficult for him because the loss of his Grandpa is still so raw and I want to be as supportive as I can.

We're entering the main hub of Boston, Newbury Street, where the world's best music store exists. Newbury Comics is where I bought my first Backstreet Boys CD so they will always have my undying support. Newbury Street is buzzing, even at 8 o'clock in the morning on a Saturday. One thing I've always loved about Boston is the eclectic mix of its residents. In Perkins Harbor people are pretty much the same, but here, you have people from all walks of life. A couple I'd never see in Perkins stroll arm-in-arm along the sidewalk. But it's not their alabaster skin with silver pierces all over it or dark ripped jeans that catches my eye. I can't stop staring at the tattoos that are covering both of their arms completely. There are a few people in Perkins with tattoos but they're small and hidden. No one broadcasts their rebellion to the world like some of the people in Boston do and I love it. Here me and my brace blend in with the rest of the metal covered bodies and faces of the unique personalities of Boston's residents.

We pass by a Starbucks and the Puma store where I bought a pair of sneakers during my family's last trip here because the ones I had brought with me had gotten caught between the teeth of a playful Rottweiler. We head out of the hub and continue on our way toward Forest Hills Avenue where the cemetery is. As we approach the gates into Forest Hills Cemetery Jamie squeezes my hand and looks at me with a half-smile.

The cemetery is broken into sections, which are grouped together by the family's last name. Since Grandpa James was Mr. Clarke's father we don't have to drive through too many of the sections to find his grave.

"There it is," Jamie says, pointing to a cobble headstone in the corner of the "C" section, with flowers sprinkled on it.

As we approach James Clarke's grave, I am very careful as to where I step, knowing that someone's family member is lying beneath my feet. I cling to Jamie's arm and kiss him as we stand in front of all that is left of his Grandfather.

I've never thought of Jamie as vulnerable but today is different. His eyes are slanted and his face flushed. He won't look at me, he just stares at the headstone that reads

JAMES CLARKE, LOVING HUSBAND AND FATHER.

"FIGHT UNTIL YOU DIE OR LIVE TRYING."

"Hey Gramps," Jamie says. "See, I promised I'd be back." His voice cracks as he places a piece of paper under one of the flowers that has already been left by an earlier visitor. I don't know what is on the paper, I didn't even know he had it, but it's folded in the same way the note he gave me was when he asked me to be his girlfriend. "I've also brought company." He looks at me and I almost don't recognize his eyes. They're usually vibrant and alive but right now they're glazed and moist. "This is April, my girlfriend. Yes, I actually have a girlfriend. She's pretty awesome and is going to be a world famous author and she is without a doubt the best person I know."

"Hello," I say and wave at the headstone. Lame girlfriend move right there. Who waves at a headstone? We didn't have a burial for my grandma Maggie. She was cremated and placed in an urn that is sitting on the mantel of our fireplace and when Amber's aunt died I stayed in the back of the crowd and never saw the headstone so I really don't know how to act around it. Jamie treated it like his Grandfather is sitting on top of it. I look around and see other graves have visitors and they're all talking to their deceased loved ones as well. "I am sorry I never had the chance to meet you but Jamie has told me wonderful things about you."

I wish I had known the man who Jamie says made him who he is today. I would love to thank James for molding his grandson to be the everything that I have been looking for in life. I don't want to cry because then Jamie will be taking care of me and today is about him and what he needs. I have felt like our entire relationship until today has been about me and now it's his turn.

"Mom and dad are doing just fine and we've adapted to life in Perkins Harbor pretty easily. It's a lot different than Boston though. The beach is really nice, not much different from Revere but there are definitely more seagulls flying around. You would have laughed last week when mom and I were down at the beach, one of the seagulls chased after her because it wanted the bagel she was eating."

"Yeah, the Perkins seagulls can be pretty vicious when it comes to food," I interject.

Jamie smiles and sits on the ground, pretty much on top of his grandfather. He crosses his legs and pulls me down next to him. *I am sitting on top of a grave. There's a person under here. This is so weird. Don't think about it and just focus on Jamie. This is what he needs so suck it up.*

"You know how you felt about Grandma? That's how I feel about April," Jamie continues. "She's the one, Gramps and even though you're not physically with me anymore I wanted you to meet her and see why I've been so happy lately. I don't have proof but I know that you had a hand in all of this so thank you for bringing her to me."

I wrap my arms around Jamie's waist and I can feel his shoulders shaking a little bit. He's crying and it's weird seeing it. I feel like I should be doing more than just rubbing his back but I don't know what to do. I have dealt with death before and have had people comfort me but I never had to be the one to comfort someone else. With Amber I used jokes and her own personality to get her through her aunt's death, but I can't do that with Jamie. So I'll just be his shoulder to cry on.

We stayed at the cemetery for a long time. After my initial discomfort I warmed up and even had a few one-sided conversations with Grandpa James myself. With Jamie's prompting I told him about my writing and also about my Backstreet Boys obsession and the concert that we're going to this summer and how lucky I was to have found him. As I spoke I realized that it didn't seem so weird talking to the headstone and I understood why people do. It's cathartic and you do feel like the person is still there in a way.

Since we still have a few minutes before we have to head back to Perkins Harbor Jamie offers to take me to see where he grew up and of course I am dying to go. I want to see where my boyfriend grew into the sexy boy he is today, although it's weird thinking of him being anywhere else but in my life.

Before the Clarke's moved to Perkins Harbor they lived in a brownstone in Beacon Hill, a section of Boston with narrow streets that could have given a few of the steep roads in San Francisco a challenge. The cobblestone is difficult to drive on and I feel like I'm on an airplane that has hit an air pocket. Jamie's childhood home is nestled between two larger brownstones but his stands out thanks to the pale pink door that his mother insisted on having. This is my favorite house in the world because it's where Jamie lived before he found me. Across the street children are screaming and shouting as they jump on the swing sets of a small playground, I wonder if Jamie played at that park when he was their age. I imagine a young Jamie running up and down the hill completely unaware of what his life would have in store for him when he was a teenager. I wonder if we ever played together when my family would visit Boston. Okay fine that's a bit of a stretch but anything is possible.

"I hated having my friends over because of that damn door," Jamie says as we stand on the street outside the house where he spent the first 18-years of his life.

Jamie walks up to the first floor window and peeks inside. The house is dark and the curtains are drawn so he's not going to be able to see much.

"We may not be able to go inside and make out but who says we can't defile the front door a little bit." He lifts me off the ground and I wrap my legs around his back and he stumbles against the pink door. The brace makes me heavier than I should be.

The streets are coming alive as people file out of their homes. Some of them stare at us while others walk by like we don't exist. I hope the current owners don't get back before we're finished making out. We have kissed a hundred times since our first date but today it feels different, like we're more connected. I don't have the same nervous tension in my chest that I had every other time. Jamie is holding me closer than normal and he's more genteel about it. It's the first time, since Halloween, that we've kissed and I don't feel like it might lead to something more. Something has changed but I know it's a good change not one that is going to end with me curled in a ball on my bed buried beneath crumbled tissues.

Jamie kisses me three times as small pecks and leans away from me. "April," he whispers, "I need you to know something. I still haven't gotten used to the fact that my grandfather is gone and coming here has always been really hard for me but having you with me today, well it is the first time I feel like I can start to let go." He smiles and allows me to hug him and brush his hand with my hand. "Thank you for today."

Until today I always felt like I needed Jamie more than he needed me. He's always coming to my rescue when people make fun of my brace and he's always there to pick up the pieces when I'm struggling with life. Today I realized that he needs me as much as I need him.

19

Marlo wasn't going to fall in love because she knew no one could love her back. She was destined to fight alien-like creatures who sought to destroy the earth and everyone on it, and this meant that anyone she cared about would be at risk. ~~Besides, who would love a girl that disappears every time they put their brace on?~~ She was determined to live in solitude but the moment Marlo met Clarke all of her plans changed.

I had the book planned out in my head. I knew how it would start, where it would climax and how it would end. I knew that Marlo would come face-to-face with The Metals, her enemies, and would come close to death before defeating them. I knew that she would struggle with the powers her brace gave her and even knew that she would lose all of her friends because of it but what I didn't know is that there would be a Clarke. I thought giving someone like Marlo a love interest wouldn't be believable because of the way she looked but I also thought having a love interest of my own wasn't believable either. I keep expecting to wake up and realize that my entire relationship with Jamie has been one long dream.

"April Rose Marks," my mother calls from downstairs. "Turn that computer off and get your butt to school!"

I have been writing since 5 o'clock a.m. when my muse decided that I no longer needed to sleep. She's a fickle creature and always pops up at the most inopportune times. Last week she paid me a visit right in the middle of a pop quiz and rather than writing about the Periodic Table I was jotting down notes about Marlo's subway adventure. Still, when she's gone I long for the random visits she gives me. I could probably write all day if going to school were optional.

I begrudgingly power off the computer and throw my red hoodie over my head and race downstairs where mom is impatiently waiting for me.

"You know mom, there is a saying among authors...never disrupt a writer at work or you might be a murder victim in their next novel."

"I guess I'll have to take my chances," mom replies as she shoves me out the door. "Happy Valentine's Day, April!"

The Flower Committee is already handing out the first batch of Valentine's as I make my way through the hallway. Principal Weist, after a lot of begging from Liza, implemented the Valentine's Flower Committee where students could send roses to their boyfriends, girlfriends, crushes, etc. throughout the day.

Amber and I used to despise Valentine's Day and rather than partaking in the festivities we would rent slasher movies and do a gory movie marathon. "This day should be banned from life," Amber had said one year after a fierce breakup with one of her boyfriends. I never had a boyfriend for Valentine's Day (Charlie and I started dating after it had passed), so I didn't mind joining Amber's bitter parade. "Seriously! Hallmark needs to find a new way to make their money," I replied. Of course, once Amber found a new boyfriend she changed her tune and now it's my turn.

"Hey Ape," April says as she skips towards me hugging a bouquet of flowers.

"I see Alex got started early," I reply flicking a dead pedal off one of the roses. "Did he send those to your house?"

"He dropped them off this morning," Amber replies, sniffing the flower like she's trying to inhale its scent.

Alex visits Amber almost every morning before school. He doesn't seem as concerned with getting to class on time as he is with spending as much time with Amber as he can. I used to envy their relationship but now, secretly, I sort of hope they envy me and Jamie's.

"Happy Valentine's Day ladies!" Liza says as she struts over to us holding a stack of cardboard hearts. The Valentines. I wonder how many are in there for me from Jamie. "Don't tell anyone but I snuck a peek at the cards and would you believe it, there are fifteen for me. Looks like I am going to get a workout carrying all those flowers around."

Amber rolls her eyes. Liza said the same thing last year when she "snuck a peek" at the cards to tally up how many were for her, the only difference was that last year she was dating Daniel

Leigh. I am sure that next year it will be someone new giving her Valentines bragging rights.

"April, do you want me to see how many are for you? I am sure there is at least one in there from your secret admirer." Liza air quotes and nods towards Amber.

She has always had it out for Amber, who she sees as competition but she's always ignored me until Jamie and I got together. Last month when Jamie and I were making out by his locker in- between classes, Liza threw Jeremy against the parallel wall and basically turned his lips into a lollipop and kept looking in our direction to see if we were paying attention. She's pissed because Jamie is hot and chose me, someone Liza considers to be at the very bottom of the popularity totem pole.

"I am sure you're getting a ton of Valentines from Jamie," Amber says to me as if Liza isn't standing in front of us." Liza is probably not telling you because she's embarrassed that you're getting more flowers than she is."

"Excuse me?" Liza says as she sashays her hips and crosses her arms.

"Oh, Liza I am sorry I didn't see you there," Amber retorts.

Amber laughs wildly throwing her head back and grabs my arm and pulls me away. "Let's go we're going to be late for class."

The tomato formerly known as Mrs. Honor is not someone I would have pegged as being *this* into Valentine's Day. I almost don't recognize the classroom. It looks as though cupid gave birth in here. The chalkboard is covered with red chalk and big lettering that reads, HAPPY VALENTINE'S DAY! LET LOVE SHINE! Paper hearts climb the walls and hang from the ceiling.

I slide into my desk and am greeted with a box of candy hearts. I look around the room and realize that all of the desks have them. "When did she have time to do all of this?" I say to Debra Milton who shrugs and takes the seat in front of me. It's the first and only thing I've ever said to her.

When Amber and I went on our "we hate Valentine's Day" binge the only thing we allowed ourselves to do that was love related was to eat those candy hearts. I always ended up getting the ones that said, "HUG ME!" or "BE MINE!"

I tear open the box and pour a few onto my desk. "I LOVE U!" and "KISS ME!" that's new. I really don't know why Amber and I loved these things so much, I might as well be chewing on chalk.

"Happy Valentine's Day everyone!" Mrs. Honor sings as the last of the stragglers take their seats. Where is Jamie? "I hope everyone gets a Valentine today but if you don't there's no need to feel rejected. "She adds. "Yeah tell that to the loser who walks out of school today flowerless," Emily Duke teases. Everyone chuckles.

Emily will get a few Valentine's from Steven McCarthy. Last year he sent her nine, one in every class.

Mrs. Honor rolls her eyes and starts scribbling hearts on the chalkboard next to the quote, "It doesn't matter who you are or what you look like, so long as somebody loves you," - Roald Dahl, *The Witches.*[1]

Jamie's face pops into my head. I can't believe how lucky I am to have him. There's no one else in the world who would be able to see me for who I am and not just for what I look like.

---

[1] "The Witches" Roald Dahl, 1983 (Puffin)

"Damnit, Jamie where are you?" I whisper to myself.

The Valentines are delivered either in the beginning of the period or near the end, which means I have only a few more minutes until I found out how many, if any, flowers Jamie ordered for me or I have almost an hour. Is that why he isn't here? Did he not order anything for me? Everyone knows we're together but if he doesn't send me any Valentine's rumors will start to spread that Jamie finally got tired of dating the "Robo-Alien."

"Since today is a day dedicated to love I am going to be doing something a little different than the lesson I originally planned "Mrs. Honor says pulling out a box from beneath her desk. "Last night I scoured the Internet in search of a book about romance and I've found something you're really going to enjoy." Donald Knight, Nicholas Austin and Baron Klein, of the Perkins Harbor High Wrestling team, groan. "Enough of that boys or it's a five page essay on The Notebook for you!"

The boys quickly shut up as Mrs. Honor begins to pass out copies of *He's Just Not That into You* paperbacks. Snickers and confused whispers move around the class. "How is that about romance?" Emily Duke asks Meredith Hass, who rolls her finger around a loose strand of hair. "Yo! It's the book I wrote to all my stalkers in the freshman class!" Jackson Lincoln whispers to his friend and slaps him five.

I stare at Jamie's empty chair next to me. I thought I'd be on cloud nine today. I thought we'd be walking through the hallways hand-in-hand, with me carrying the bouquet of roses that Jamie got for me. This does not feel like Valentine's Day.

"Miss Marks," Mrs. Honor says, placing a copy of the book on my desk. "Did you hear what the assignment was?" Of course, I didn't. I was too busy zoning out on Jamie's empty desk to realize that Mrs. Honor had even gotten to my aisle. I shake my head, no. She touches my shoulder comfortingly. "It's just another day in the month." I want to say, "Yeah, tell that to my broken heart," but instead I just smile.

Knock, knock, knock. "Valentine's Delivery!" Liza sings as she and two trembling freshmen girls stalk into the room carrying five bouquets of flowers in each hand. All the girls, including me, scoot up in their chairs.

Liza and the nervous girls make their way through the aisles. Handing out flowers.

"Three bouquets for you Emily." Emily takes her flowers and waves them around while bouncing in her chair. "And Donald here's two flowers...and even Mary Highland, well I do believe I have one for you too!" (Mary was voted least-likely to get a boyfriend by Liza and her lackeys.). The girls split up from Liza and make their way down the end and center aisles and Liza struts down mine. She stops in front of me and smiles as she pulls out the last three roses.

"April, these are for..." Liza says, as she holds out the roses. The spinning cycle in my stomach stops and my heart settles down. Jamie came through. I can finally breathe again. "Debra Milton. Where does she sit?"

I can hear my heart shattering as Liza's lips start to slide up toward her ears. I feel like a pathetic reminder of what a loser looks like.

"What's that?" Emily shouts.

She's staring at the door, her eyes slanted and her mouth cocked to the side. Liza, still grinning maliciously at me, looks up and her jaw drops. The boys burst into tears of laughter and Mrs. Honor, who has frozen at the chalkboard, blinks rapidly at the door.

"Oh my God!" I blurt out. Cupid is standing in the doorway and he is dressed like Jamie!

"Sorry I'm late but I accidentally shot the wrong person in the butt with one of my arrows and well, let's just say what they're about to do is illegal in almost all of the 50 states," cupid Jamie says as he adjusts the cloth drooping down on his hips, the only thing that he is wearing!

"Mr. Clarke!" Mrs. Honor shouts. "Go home and put some clothes on!"

"Please, call me Cupid," Jamie says, as he gives me a quick wink. "I am here to deliver these flowers to that beautiful angel sitting in the back."

Everyone is looking at me but the only person I can see is Jamie. He looks like the baby from the *Roger Rabbit* cartoons and still he's is the most beautiful creature I've ever seen. He struts towards me, and plies every few steps. He looks ridiculous but wonderful. My stomach is back on its spin cycle and sweat drips down my back as Jamie reaches my desk.

"Mr. Clarke!" Mrs. Honor shouts as she slams her hand on her desk.

"Jamie, what are you doing?" I whisper to him.

"Giving my girl the Valentine's Day she deserves," Jamie replies as he hands me the flowers.

"You could have just sent me a Valentine," I say, as I blush from ear to ear.

"Yes, I could have but this is so much better, don't you think?"

"You're crazy, Jamie Clarke."

"And you're beautiful, April Marks," Jamie replies as he heads towards the classroom door.

"Mr. Clarke! " Ms. Honor is furious. "Get out of my classroom before I have you suspended from this school!"

As Jamie exits the classroom the boys are roaring with laughter, the girls are as red as their flowers, Liza is speechless and me, I feel like her Royal Highness of Valentine's Day!

20

It's Easter vacation and despite Principal Weist suspending Jamie for three days for the whole Cupid incident, things have been relatively quiet around here; well except for the fact that Jamie has been planning something special for the six month anniversary of our first date but the bastard won't tell me what it is. I have tried to pry the plan out of him but the boy just won't budge. "Have patience," is all he says when I ask for a hint and when I hit him with the, "please I'll love you forever" gambit it doesn't work because he already knows I will.

I have no clue what to wear! Do I wear my typical blue jeans, a blouse with some sort of pattern on it and flats? Or is this a heels kind of a place? I look at the heap of clothing that I have thrown into the reject pile on my bed. My parents have agreed to let me leave the brace off for the night. "But the minute you get home that brace goes on," says mom as she relents. Even brace-free I can't find anything acceptable to wear.

"Crud!" I shout as I launch another reject onto the growing

pile.

"April, you okay in there?"

"I'm fine mom,"

"April, are you nervous about tonight?" mom asks, poking

her head into the room.

"I said I'm fine mom," I reply impatiently. "Please just go

back downstairs."

But instead she waltzes in like I gave her an invitation to.

Why do mothers have to do that? It's like they have their

own way of hearing things and usually it isn't the way you

actually said it. My mother is the queen of selective hearing.

Last year on the first day of school, even though I have my

own car, she asked me if I wanted a ride. "Mom! that is so

uncool," I had explained. However, since my mother has that

selective hearing problem she insisted on driving me. "I'll

just drop you off. No one will even know I am there," she

promised. But in true motherly fashion, when we got to

school she pulled up in front of the building where everyone saw me getting out of my *Mommy's* car. What's worse is they saw her give me a kiss and a pat on the head as she said, "Good luck on your first day." So humiliating!

"Are you nervous about tonight?" mom asks as she searches through the rejection pile as if I hadn't already done that a dozen times.

"No and please come in," I say flatly as I continue to unload the contents of the middle drawer of my dresser.

"You've been with Jamie for six months now, right?" I nod. "Then there's nothing to worry about because if he hasn't gone running for the hills by now he's sticking around, no matter how crappy your clothing selection might be."

Mom always knows how to provoke me. Like right now a normal mother would talk me down from my irrational conclusion that I have nothing to wear by reassuring me that Jamie loves me for me, not my clothing. But not my mother no, she thinks teasing me and making sarcastic comments is the way to go. I really wish Amber wasn't away right now visiting her grandmother in Toronto. Her parents have the worst timing ever. Why does she have to be out of state when I am having a crisis and the only person giving me any "comfort" is my crazy mother?

"Thanks for the sound advice mom. It's nice to know I can always count on you to make me feel better," I retort sarcastically.

Mom sits on the bed and places her hand on the clothing pile. Her lips and eyebrows flatten and as her shoulders roll I know that her "serious voice" is on its way, which is really just a deeper version of her normal British accented voice.

Mom moved from England to the States when she met and fell in love with my father, who was doing a semester abroad. That kind of devotion astounds me. Picking up your entire life for someone else, I mean that's true love. What would I do if Jamie asked me to pick up everything and follow him to another country? I couldn't imagine being without him so why not right? Mom did it when she was my age and I've never seen two people happier and more in love (aside from me and Jamie of course) than my parents are. Besides isn't the statement, "Love conquers all?"

"Honey, these are just material items they're not what makes you, you. Jamie didn't fall in love with your clothing or your hair or those beautiful eyes of yours, he fell in love with *you*. If Jamie is the kind of person your father and I think he is, and the kind of person you've said he is, then you could walk out of here in sweats and he'd think you were the most beautiful girl in the world," mom says with a smile. Finally! There's the normal mother I always knew she could be!

She's right. I know she's right but I've never had a six-month anniversary celebration before. When Charlie and I reached our six-month mark neither of us acknowledged it. I didn't because I was already thinking of ways to break up with him and he didn't because he was thinking of all the ways to tell me he was in love with me. So this is a really big deal.

"I know, mom but he didn't even tell me what type of place we're going to. What if we're going to some incredibly upscale, hoity-toity place and I end up wearing jeans and this blouse." I pick up a black blouse with a bright red rose embroidered in the center of it, "and everyone laughs at me or we get kicked out?"

"Then you'll go somewhere else where you can fit in with the rest of the riffraff."

"Mom!" I whine and throw myself in the middle of the rejection mountain. I clamp my hands over my mouth and scream.

"Yes, let it out and once you're done overreacting we'll look through this pile together and find you something perfect to wear."

I hate to admit it and I doubt I ever will again but mom is right; I am overreacting and if Jamie knew how stressed out his surprise was making me he would feel horrible and the entire night would be ruined. I calm down and we begin searching through the pile.

"How about this?" mom says holding up a lemon colored sweater.

"You're joking, right?" I reply and she tosses the reject over her shoulder.

We've successfully moved half of the pile onto the floor behind us and I'm once again losing hope. "This is useless," I wine.

"Wait a minute, I think we have a winner!" mom sings as she holds out a red blouse and grey slacks with matching charcoal jacket. Yes!

"Okay next problem. Hair up or down?" I ask as I hold my hair up and then let it fall as option number two.

"Down," Mom says grabbing something off the top of my dresser. "But put this in to give it a little something extra."

She hands me the blue butterfly hairclip that Grandma Maggie gave me when I was seven. It was mom's birthday and we were getting ready to go out to dinner. I was complaining about my hair and how flat it always looked. "I look like Cousin It!" I screamed, stomping my feet around the house. Grandma Maggie marched me into her bedroom and pulled the clip off her dresser and pulled two sections of my hair together and shoved the clip in. "There now you look like your beautiful self," she had said as the clip snapped in place. I looked in the mirror and fell in love with the hair clip and the way I looked with it. "Cousin It is no more!" I had shouted while I danced around the room.

When we went home I conveniently forgot to give the clip back to Grandma Maggie and now it's become a memorial piece. My parents refer to it as our new family heirloom.

"There, perfect," my mother says as she admires her work in the mirror.

Her work being me of course. Sometimes I wonder: is my mother more pleased with herself for creating me or with the person I have become? I suppose either way it's a good thing. I stare at my reflection. I know what Jamie says about me, that I'm "beautiful," and "breathtaking," but I don't see it. Mom must see it too because she is smiling so wide I can see her gums. She cups my shoulders and lowers her face so it is next to mine. We have the same dark eyes and the same chocolate hair, though hers has a tint of silver. She has a lot more wrinkles than I do. Well, actually I don't have any at all, but a few more nights of anxiety and I am sure that is bound to change.

"Mom, how did you know dad was *the one*?" I ask as I try to wiggle away from the mirror. I am tired of looking at myself.

"What do you mean, sweetheart?" mom asks.

"How did you know that dad was the one? You know the big kahuna, the one who completes you and all." I reply and grab my bedazzled clutch purse off the dresser.

"Well, as your mother I'm supposed to lie to you and tell you that there isn't just one thing that made me realize that he was the one but…I will tell you the exact moment I knew your father was it, the big kahuna," mom says as she flops down on my bed. "We had been dating for a little less than a year and I had stayed over one night after a Bon Jovi concert."

Picturing my parents rocking out to Bon Jovi is just weird. Mom in ripped jeans, a band t-shirt and multi-colored hair and dad with a Mohawk, multiple piercings and 'guy-liner,' come on its too good not to make fun of.

"Bon Jovi? Nice," I tease and throw up my index and pinky finger to make devil horns.

"Well, excuse me. Not all of us enjoy watching a bunch of men bouncing around stage in-synchronization and singing cheesy love songs, April," Mom laughs. "Now, do you want to hear the story or not?" I nod for her to continue. "Your father and I spent the night together…no not like that so you can relax that disgusted face of yours. When I woke up the next morning your father was still sleeping. I watched him sleep and it was the most peaceful I'd ever felt, lying there watching him sleep. That's the moment I realized that the idea of waking up next to him every day for the rest of my life was something I definitely wanted. In fact, the idea of not being with him for the rest of life was not a life I wanted to even consider," mom says. She is smiling so contently she has to be reliving that moment with dad in her mind.

She is waiting for a reaction from me but this isn't the story I was expecting. I assumed she would tell me some epic story about how their eyes met and her heart fluttered and she knew that her life was complete. But instead I got a story about how she creepily watched my father sleep and then mentally married him.

"Oh," I reply trying to mask my disappointment. "Okay."

"Why do you ask?"

There is no way I am going to tell her. If she knew what Jamie and I discussed on Christmas Eve she'd flip out and say things like, "Are you crazy? You're too young to get married!" or worse, "Are you pregnant?" which according to my father is the only reason "Young people get married these days." I tell my mother a lot but I think this I'll keep to myself for a little while longer.

"No reason. I was just curious," I lie hoping she won't notice.

"Okay, well whenever you decide to tell me the truth I'm around."

Ding dong! Jamie is right on time as always. I never get any extra time. Would a little tardiness kill him?

21

We've been driving for over an hour and we still haven't reached our destination. I'm beginning to think Jamie has no idea where he's going. We're driving on some backwoods road with nothing but trees surrounding us. Mother Nature has brought in fog and I feel like I'm in the middle of a *Twilight* movie and Robert Pattinson is going to jump in front of the car at any moment.

"If you turn into a vampire right now I'm going to be really pissed off," I tease as Jamie negotiates a sharp turn.

"Don't worry I only drink the blood of the innocent and you, my dear, are far from that," Jamie retorts.

I nudge his shoulder and stick out my tongue at him and it gives me more time to admire how handsome he is in that white button down, black slack and a blue tie outfit. Obviously we're going someplace nice. This isn't his typical I-don't-have-a-style-wear and I know how uncomfortable he is in this kind of semi-formal wear. It makes me smile knowing that even though he hates it, he does it for me. Amber is the type of person who gets the boys like this. Although she's never had a truly long-term relationship she has always had her boyfriends wrapped around her finger.

"Seriously, Jamie where the heck are you taking me?"

"I told you. It's a surprise so you will have to wait."

"Can you give me a hint? I mean will there at least be civilization?"

"Okay, I'll give you a hint if you send me your book." And that puts an end to that! I recently, by some miracle, have been able to get within a few paragraphs of finishing the book. But there is no way I am letting Jamie see it. He's been bugging me for days about it but it's the first thing I've ever really written and I don't want my boyfriend reading something that is anything less than perfect. "I figured as much," Jamie says as he turns the dial on the radio.

He's been playing with the radio ever since we got in the car. He has very eclectic musical tastes. The last time I was in his car I went through his box of CDs and saw everything from The Doors to Britney Spears and he had even purchased the newest Backstreet

Boys CD for me. Secretly I wonder if he bought it so *he* could listen to it when I wasn't around.

"You should probably put on one of your thousand CDs. You have been messing with the radio since we left my house and haven't found a decent station yet."

"Fine, Miss Music Genius, why don't you pick out something?"

"Okay, but remember you told me to," I tease as I grab the Backstreet Boys CD.

"Wow I had no idea you'd pick that one," Jamie says sarcastically.

I blow a raspberry at him and allow myself to fall into the music. Maybe it will make this never ending car ride seem less like the beginning of a horror movie and more like a romantic evening. And if it's not then at least, if I survive, I'll have another book to write.

"We're here," Jamie sings as he puts the car in park.

"Where's here? I can't see anything but darkness," I reply.

I recall a horror movie Jamie and I watched a few days ago about a couple who was lured out into the middle of nowhere for some secret party but when the couple arrived they were both slaughtered by the people living in the forest. When your boyfriend drives you to the middle of nowhere at night and you see no signs of civilization, you can't help but let your mind wander.

"Trust me," Jamie says and exits the car to makes his way around to my door. "You trust me, right?"

I do.

The restaurant is surrounded by a dense display of trees and shrubbery. It's only about a five minute walk from the car to the restaurant but I am close to sending out a distress signal. Spiders greet us as they dangle from their webs and each time I see one I squeal and Jamie rumbles with laughter. I'm relieved that our woodsy adventure is over. The gravelly parking lot is filled, which means this place is going to be good.

"This is the first and last time I'll ever interact that much with nature!" I shout as I shake off a moth that has taken up residence on my arm.

"Sorry about the trek but I wanted to keep a certain element of surprise to the night," Jamie says. "Plus you look really cute when you're running away from a bug. "As he wraps his arms around me we enter the small log cabin with the twinkling lights and enormous trees surrounding it and a sign that reads "Nana's Little Paradise."

22

"We're like the youngest people in here" I whisper to Jamie." Are you sure this isn't a restaurant for a nursing home or something?"

I can smell the food being cooked inside. Garlic, rosemary and cooked tomatoes fill the air as we enter a small foyer where the hostess stands. The interior of the restaurant is not at all how I thought it would be. Tables spread out from front to back covering nearly every inch of the dining room. The room is flowing with conversation.

A petite woman with spiral golden hair greets us. "Good Evening and welcome to Nana's Little Paradise. Do you have a reservation?"

"Yes, under Clarke," Jamie says glancing at the reservation book.

I can't believe how many names are on the reservation list there must be at least twenty or so. How can this place be so popular when I've never heard of it before? I know every popular restaurant within a 50 mile radius of my home. Amber and I stayed up one night looking up stupid things, popular restaurants in Maine being one of them, and I didn't see this place on the lists that Google came back with.

The hostess checks the book and stops midway down the page. "Ah, Mr. Clarke - table for two. Right this way."

She grabs two leather bound menus and leads us to a table in the far right corner of the restaurant. It's private and pushed away from the rest of the filled restaurant. When he made the reservation Jamie must have told them it was for a special occasion because our table is the only one with a votive candle floating in a heart shaped pool of water surrounded by rose petals. Jamie pulls the chair out for me and I slide onto the cushion. It is more comfortable than it looks. The hostess hands me the menu and does the same when Jamie takes his seat across from me.

I keep glancing back and forth between the Chicken Picatta and the Penne ala vodka. Both seem equally delicious and if I were with my parents I'd probably order both and take any leftovers, not that there would be, home.

This is an Italian restaurant and it's my favorite type of food. Jamie did exceptionally well with this choice.

"Everything looks so good," Jamie says from behind his menu. "I'm not sure I can decide on just one dish."

"I was just thinking the same thing," I am relieved that he is as hungry as I am.

"Well maybe we can help one another out. Let's pick out our top three dishes and share them. How does that sound?"

I'm supposed to be the dainty girl in the relationship who is sometimes sophisticated but always girly. If I agree to this deal then I know I'll end up eating more than Jamie and he'll think I'm a fatty. Amber always says that guys don't like a girl who can eat more than they can. It makes us look like we're just a few meals away from obesity. Eventually I am sure I will learn not to listen to everything Amber says about boys.

"Oh, I don't know if I can eat that much but if you want to order more than one dish I promise not to judge you," I reply. What a load of crap.

Jamie cocks his head and gives me a crooked smile as the waitress introduces herself.

"Welcome to Nana's. My name is Margaret and I will be your waitress this evening. Are you ready to order?"

"Not just yet" Jamie says putting on a slight British accent. My mother would be so proud.

"Take your time. I'll be back," she says as she waddles away.

Jamie browses the menu and taps his finger on the glass in front of him. "CLINK"! His glass tumbles off the table and shatters into fragments. "Don't worry, I've got it" says one of the busboys who is standing to the side as everyone turns to see who the loud culprits are. We should be embarrassed but instead we burst into uncontrollable laughter. "You would think they could be more well-mannered" we hear a middle-aged couple say as they stare at us from the next table.

"We're like freaks at a circus" Jamie says to me.

"I know", I reply; "the ones who have two heads and six limbs. I've been to fancy restaurants before. When I was fourteen-years-old my parents took me to Disneyworld for my birthday and booked us a table at Victoria & Albert's, you know, a five-star gourmet restaurant in the Grand Floridian Hotel. There was a dress code and a seven-course meal. It was a luxury I wasn't used to but even there, surrounded by wealthy adults, I still felt less judged than I do tonight".

Margaret returns to take our order.

"They're just jealous of us," says Jamie.

As I go to pick up my water glass Jamie says "Whoa, whoa! What are you doing? "Placing his hand over my glass he says "you can't drink yet. First we have to make a toast."

"Are you ready to order now?" Margaret asks.

"Yes, I think we are, right April?"

"Yup, I'm good," I reply and turn toward Margaret. "I'll have the penne ala vodka please."

"And I'll have the chicken piccata," Jamie says gleefully as he hands Margaret the menu.

As our waitress shuffles away Jamie raises his glass and it's time to toast. I raise mine but I'm a little too anxious and end up spilling some of it on the back of my hand.

"Here's to you and the past six months of our lives together and here's to having many more anniversaries in the years to come," Jamie toasts and pauses and looks at me with those blue eyes. Ugh those eyes. "So tell me honestly, why you won't let me read your book?" he asks setting his glass down.

"Jamie," I whine. "I told you it's not ready."

"But you said it's almost done, right?" I nod. "Okay, so you promised that once it was you'd let me read it and I think almost done is close enough. It doesn't have to be edited or anything. Trust me I won't judge you. Besides you've seen the essays Mrs. Honor assigns us, they read like a five-year-olds journal. I am sure your book is great."

He's incredibly persuasive but if I show him the book he'll think its crap and then any confidence he had that I could become a New York Times Bestselling author will disappear. He'll become another naysayer and I can't handle that.

"No, Jamie, not yet. I promise as soon as I think it's good enough to be read you'll be the first person who reads it but for now trust me when I say it's not ready."

"Let's call this a difference of opinion then," Jamie says pouting. "But you can't keep your work hidden forever, April."

"I know and I promise you *will* be the first person who gets to read it."

Jamie winks and mouths, "Promise?" I nod.

"So did you hear Erik is having a big party tomorrow night?" Jamie asks.

Shit! I think I'd rather go back to talking about my book.

23

Erik Marshall was the first friend, aside from me, that Jamie made when he first arrived in Perkins Harbor. When Jamie isn't with me he is at Erik's either playing video games or some sort of sport. Erik's parents are also loaded. His dad owns half of the shops in The Cove and his mother won some big settlement in court when she sued her ex-husband for slander. He is one of the "popular kids," and before Jamie came along he was the hottest guy in school and every girl, including myself, had a crush on him.

After Jamie and I became a couple his friendship with Erik was a little awkward for me. Last year I told Penny Hamill, my art partner, that I had a crush on Erik. Big mistake because immediately after class ended she ran to tell him and before the day had ended the entire school knew. I couldn't look in his direction for months. Now that Jamie and I are together and he and Erik are close friends its only natural that our paths should cross again, although I have done a good job of avoiding it. Each time Jamie will ask if I want to go with him to hang out with Erik I will come up with some believable excuse not to go and for the two parties that Jamie was able to convince me to go to I found a way to avoid seeing Erik.

"April, did you hear me?" Jamie asks. "About Erik's party?"

"I feel like he is always having a party of some kind. It's Friday let's celebrate. Oh I just got an A on a paper, time for a party! That kid has every excuse to throw a party and his parents never say anything to him. I don't get it," I reply.

"Any interest in going?" Jamie asks, his voice filled with hope.

As much as he claims he doesn't care about Erik's parties I know that he does. Erik always has some kind of spiked drink and a lot of fried-greasy foods, something Jamie doesn't get a lot of at home. His parents are health nuts and only allow organic and good-for-you foods in their home. Even his dog, Diogee, is given all natural foods. I think Jamie is embarrassed by the fact that his parents haven't exactly left "hippie-dumb," as he puts it. I don't think my parents have escaped "hippie-dumb," either. They're all about love, peace and living in the world as one. It's a little strange considering their teenage years of rock and roll, sex and drugs. So far Jamie's parents don't seem like the type to go on about love, peace and living as one.

"Oh, I don't know," I reply as I browse the room hoping to see the waitress bringing our food over. I want a distraction. Every new party we go to is one more step closer to having to talk to Erik and make an awkward situation ten times worse.

"Do you not want to go?"

"No, it's not that I don't want to," I allow my voice to trail off.

Jamie's face contorts. He's disappointed. I hate disappointing him. It is just as bad as when you do something wrong at home and your parents say, 'I'm not mad, I'm disappointed.'

"Then what is it?"

Do I just suck it up and tell him the truth? I mean it was practically two years ago that I had a crush on Erik it means nothing now. I'm not the first girl Jamie ever liked or dated. He had a past just like I do and neither of us can put the other at fault for anything we did before we met, right? But it could make things more awkward if I tell Jamie the truth. If he knows that I used to have a crush on his best friend it could ruin their friendship. But if he finds out from someone else he'll think I was keeping it from him on purpose and this will lead to suspicion that I'm not over Erik.

Oh thank God. "Here we are. Penne ala vodka for the young lady and Chicken picatta for the gentleman," Margaret says as she puts our dishes in front of us.

I move some of the more overcooked pieces of pasta around on the plate before I take my first bite. I knew it. It tastes even better than it smells. The sharpness of the tomato sauce mixed with the tangy flavor of the cooked vodka is intoxicating.

"So," Jamie says taking a bite of his chicken, "why don't you want to go to Erik's party? Do you not like him or something?"

Damn, damn, damn he didn't forget. I have to tell him the truth, I suppose. This sucks! I can't even remember why I had a crush on Erik in the first place.

"Okay, but if I tell you please promise that you won't get mad and weird."

"Mad and weird about what?"

My stomach is like a Ferris wheel that's spinning out of control and I can taste bile building in my throat. This shouldn't be that big a deal it's not like I still have a thing for Erik. Jamie dabs his forehead with a napkin and takes a long sip of water. I take a deep breath and put my fork down and fold my hands in my lap so he doesn't see them shaking.

"Like two-years-ago, way before we met, before I knew you even existed I kind of, sort of, had a crush on," I pause trying to steady my voice. I sound like a radio with a dying battery that has been submerged in water. "Erik. I am sorry I didn't tell you sooner but I didn't want you to be mad or think that I still harbored any feelings for him, because I don't. It was a stupid and meaningless crush. And well, he found out and it was just really awkward and embarrassing. But he means nothing to me now. The only person I want to be with is you. You're more than just a crush and you know that."

I'm exhausted. Now I wait for Jamie to react, for his face to turn the color of the vodka sauce and for him to be furious with me for not telling him sooner. This is his best friend I am talking about and I know that if Jamie had had a crush on Amber before we met I'd probably be feeling pretty hurt right about now, even though I know it's silly. Still, if the roles were reversed I'd probably always be concerned that the feelings would come back and I really hope Jamie isn't feeling that way. I am expecting him to flip out and to tell me that I betrayed him or worse but he is just sitting there completely silent. I swear I see the edges of his mouth starting toward the ceiling. Is he smiling? No, he can't be. He should be angry with me and this should be the start of our second fight, right? Isn't that how these things work?

"Is that it?" Jamie asks as his lips curl upward. I nod. "Okay. Is there any way I can convince you to come with me to this party? I mean I suppose I could go without you but that wouldn't really be any fun now would it?"

Wait, what?

"Jamie, did you hear what I said before about why I don't want to go to the party?" I inquire. I am confused.

"Yes of course I heard you," Jamie replies. "I really think we'd have a good time. Plus I heard that Erik is going to have a keg and I've always wanted to see what a keg stand was."

"Wait, what? No, Jamie wait. I had a crush on Erik...your best friend, Erik you know, the boy who is throwing the party. I liked him. Liked him, liked him."

"April, I heard you. I get it. You liked him. You had a crush on him. You wanted him to be your boyfriend. I understand."
I'm still lost.

"If you understand then how could you still want me to go to the party? Why are you so calm about this?"

Jamie puts his fork down. His piercing eyes glare at me with the same intensity they had on Christmas when we were discussing the idea of marriage. "Because that is your past. Your feelings for Erik, or whatever it was, happened before we met. Why should it bother me that you had a crush on someone before you knew me? I believe we're meant to be together but I'm not a hippie like my parents and I don't believe that people sit around waiting for the *one* their whole lives without falling for a few duds first."

The cinder block of my Erik crush falls off my shoulders and I can breathe again. It is like studying super hard for a test and finding out it has been cancelled.

"So you're calling your so-called best friend a dud?" I tease as I take a spoonful of pasta. I think it tastes better than it did before.

"Erik, ha, the dude is a major dud in the world of worthy fish in your pond."

"The only fish I want swimming in my pond is you," I say winking at him.

I don't really have a curfew but my parents prefer it if I am home by midnight on weekends and by ten on schooldays. I don't fight them on this because usually I am exhausted and ready for bed by eleven anyway. Tonight however, as we pull up to my house I can't help but wish it wasn't 11:57 p.m., I really don't want to put that damn brace back on. Besides, tonight seems like it would be the perfect night for...*you-know-what*. Jamie puts the car into park and looks at me. Can't just for a few minutes, he not be so cute?

"I hope you had a good time tonight," Jamie says as he pushes a piece of hair behind my ear.

"Are you kidding? Tonight was perfect," I reply grabbing and kissing the palm of his hand.

"Hey, you have to do the six-month celebration right. It is, after all, the halfway mark to the year anniversary and that's when things get really interesting."

"Seriously, Jamie I had a great time tonight. The food was amazing and that Tiramisu...I am definitely going to dream about that tonight."

Jamie frowns playfully. "Look I'm up for a good competition but I am not sure I'm up to battling with a Tiramisu."

"Well lucky for you I will forego the satisfaction of such a delectable dessert," I tease. "It is a difficult sacrifice to make but I think I can do it."

With a crooked smile Jamie kisses me. He runs his hands through my hair and tugs gently and makes his way for the nape of my neck. His hands are soft hands and always warm. It is a nice contrast to my own, which are permanently cold. He pulls back and kisses my neck and collarbone. I close my eyes and focus on the sensation of his lips. As wonderful as it is kissing him I am very aware of the fact that it is now midnight and if I stay in this car any longer we're going to be christening the backseat. I pull back and smile timidly.

"I should probably go inside," I say and place my hand on the side of his face. "Thank you again for a perfect evening."

As I exit the car Jamie asks, "So where did we land about Erik's party?"

I almost forgot about the stupid party.

"I guess we can go," I reply reluctantly. "Pick me up at 8?"

"Sounds good. See you tomorrow, my everything!" Jamie says through the open window before driving off.

24

I am going to Erik's but I think Jamie is going to have a hard time given what I told him last night. I have a sinking feeling about it.

Bang, bang, bang, I slap the laptop until the cooling fan buzzes and the yellow power light comes on. Jamie is helping his dad, Amber is mysteriously unavailable and the parental units are out so it's time for me to dive back into Marlo's world.

The Metals have Marlo cornered and her brace is just out of reach. She'll have to get out of this one on her own. The condensation from last night's rainstorm trickles down Marlo's back as she pulls one of the loose nails on the pipe free. Now all she needs to do is wiggle it a little and then she'll be able to use it to knock Kly out and save Clarke.

"It's over Ms. Hunch," Kly snarls. "Give in to us or these will be the last words your lover ever hears."

The devastation in Clarke's eyes as Kly tightens his tentacle around his neck sends Marlo's adrenaline into overdrive. Her heart is racing and her body is covered in sweat. If she doesn't act now her lover is doomed. As the pipe falls into her hand, Marlo lunges at Kly and...and...and...

Great! Once again I am struck down by writer's block! I have been doing everything right. I've listened to inspirational music. I've read a ton of those, *How To Write* books and I've even outlined each chapter and still I can't fend off the barricade in my mind. I was delusional to think that this would be easy. Writing stories in a journal one's fifth grade teacher gave them is a lot different than writing a full book. What was I thinking? There is no way I am ever going to submit this to any literary agencies.

Buzz, Buzz. NEW TEXT MESSAGE – AMBER:

Ape – I hope you're almost ready! I'm leaving in fifteen minutes!

Ugh! Once again I leave Marlo's world and come home to reality. I'm never going to get this book finished. I wish I hadn't agreed to go tonight.

If there is one thing Amber will never miss it's one of Erik's parties. "They are the best place to get in with the right crowd," she always says. The only time Amber came close though was when she attended one of Liza's parties (sans me) and shared a keg with Liza and her friends. Everyone was too drunk to have conversation so they just took turns doing keg stands and taking shots of whatever concoction Ralph Marlen, the football quarterback, created from the liquor cabinet. I have to give Amber credit for trying though.

"Ape!" Amber calls from downstairs. "Are you ready? Jamie is going to be here any minute."

Jamie is picking us up at 8 o'clock and Amber got here at 7:10 p.m., as I was just getting out of the shower. She lectured me for a good ten minutes about proper party night etiquette, apparently getting out of a shower and leaving only forty-minutes to get ready was a party sin. "You should be placed in party jail for this crime," Amber had said when she marched into my room and nearly startled me out of the towel I was wearing.

"Okay, okay give me a minute!" I shout.

She is so impatient with me now but when she is the one taking her time she expects me to wait quietly.

I tie back my hair and check out my outfit in the mirror. "Are you sure this blouse doesn't make me look like a Muppet?" I shout loud enough for Amber, who is waiting downstairs, to hear me. "I feel like its exposing too much of the brace!"

"April, its fine! Now let's go!" Amber demands.

"Ugh!" I smooth out the wrinkles on my jeans before heading downstairs to stop Amber from pacing a hole in the floor of the foyer.

"Finally!" Amber says stomping her foot.

"Oh lord Amber, lighten up it's one of Erik's stupid parties," I say and roll my eyes. "A bunch of drunken idiots running around, cursing, fighting, pissing everywhere and making out. Then, Liza and Jeremy will get into a fight and he'll speed off in that shit brown car of his and that will signal the end of the party."

Amber tosses me a thin shirt to bring along and heads for the door. She is really persistent tonight but last I heard Alex wasn't going to be able to make it so I don't understand why she is so anxious. The people who show up on time for high school parties include the band geeks and the mathletes. I figured we would hang out at my house for a little before heading to the party but from the looks of it Amber is going to jump in Jamie's car before it even comes to a stop.

"Why the sudden rush to get there?" I ask as I throw the shirt in my purse and follow Amber out the door.

She looks up and down the block for Jamie's car but the only thing on the block are parked cars, houses and Mrs. Martin taking her aged golden retriever Amy, for her nightly walk. Friday nights in Perkins Harbor, before the summer vacationers come, are always quiet, at least in the residential areas and there isn't much for a teenager to do around here at night. Sometimes Amber and I will walk to the beach and go for a late swim but we haven't done that since we were caught and lectured by a security guard last summer.

"What's the rush?" I repeat.

"There's no rush. I just don't want to stand around waiting for your boyfriend all night," Amber scoffs.

She is hiding something.

25

Marcy's Corner is a small gated community with mansions that would rival those in Beverly Hills. Some of them look like they should come with their own zip code. Erik lives on the very end of the block so we have to drive through a good portion of the community to get to his house. I have been here a few times but I'm still amazed at the size of these houses. For me, there is magic in the air and I swear I can hear the angels singing as a towering alabaster mansion climbs into view. It's like the universe is saying, "Look, April, it's something you'll never have."

A shadowy figure moves around inside the giant windows where fluorescent light casts a spotlight on the rose bushes that line the front side of the massive home. Jamie pulls into the crescent driveway and we park between a blue Jaguar and Erik's snot green Hummer.

"Looks like we might be the first ones here," Jamie says as we ascend the wrap-around porch.

"I swear, this house was designed directly from a Bob Ross

painting," I say as Jamie rings the doorbell. "Aw man! I forgot he had a porch swing! I wish my house were big enough to have a porch swing. The closest I ever got was the hammock my dad hung in the backyard. Remember that thing, Amber?"

The front door flies open and my former crush appears and I remember what it was I found so attractive about him. I'm one of those girls who has a weakness for light eyes that seem like they don't quite fit the muscle-man behind them. He's nothing to me now but can I really be blamed for once finding those chiseled cheekbones irresistible?

"Hey, Jay-man!" Erik says opening the front door.

This is the first time in almost two years that I am allowing him to see me.

"April Marks," Erik says as we enter the foyer with ceilings as high as the sky. "I haven't seen you since the beginning of freshman year. I mean there were rumors that you've been to some of my parties but I've never seen you. You must have been avoiding me."

"Never," I tease.

"Good. It would be pretty awkward if you were, considering you and my boy have been all hot and heavy and it was like two-years-ago."

My heart drops. I can't believe he just said that. He couldn't have been more obvious than if he said, "Remember the time you had a crush on me?" All I want to do is crawl under a rock. It was hard enough for me to bring it up with Jamie but to have Erik bring it up here, now, makes it ten times worse.

"Well, we all know I'm not avoiding you and isn't that really all that matters?" Amber chimes in.

Erik's face is flushed as turns on his heels toward my best friend.

"Hey Amber," Erik says as he places his hands in the front pockets of his jeans and lowers his head.

This is so weird. I have never, in all the years I have known him, seen Erik be shy.

I nudge Amber lightly and in true Amber fashion she smiles and mouths, *we'll talk later.*

"Where's the alcohol?" Jamie asks abruptly.

"Oh, dude I've totally gone all out for this bash," Erik says. "Every kind of alcohol you can imagine is laid out in the kitchen. Do I know how to throw a party or what?"

He throws a hand in the air and waits for Jamie to slap him five but Jamie ignores him and heads for the kitchen.

"What was that all about?" Amber asks no one in particular.

"I have no idea," I shrug but I have a feeling I know.

Erik lowers his hand slowly and scratches his head. "Well you're the first to arrive so shall we grab a drink before the hounds begin to swarm?" He leads us into the ridiculous kitchen, where Jamie is already digging through the alcohol stash.

If you've ever seen the MTV series, *Cribs,* then you've basically seen Erik's kitchen. You could put my entire first floor in this kitchen. Two buckets of beer wait for us tucked away in the breakfast nook. Alcohol bottles decorate the bay window and there is a large keg in the corner.

"So what's your poison?" Erik asks me.

"She's not a big drinker," Jamie says, pulling out a beer. "Besides I basically had to convince her to come tonight. April isn't much of a social butterfly."

Erik's eye dart through me as he and Amber share a laugh at my expense.

"Oh, okay then," Erik stammers. "I'm not really sure what I can offer you. I basically cleared out all the non-alcoholic beverages."

"I am sure water will be fine, right babe?"

"What?" I am completely taken aback by Jamie's behavior.

"I'm just saying you aren't a real party girl. This isn't your scene, so just have water. I know you would rather be home watching Backstreet Boys DVDs than hanging out at another one of these parties. Besides didn't you say you really didn't like Erik?"

Jamie has never spoken to me like this before, not even when we had that horrible fight. He's gas lighting me. He is behaving like a child. If he wasn't okay with the feelings I once had for Erik then he should have said so and I wouldn't have come tonight. He really had to wait till now to be a dick about it?

"Actually, I'll have a beer," I say and slam my hand into the bucket. The ice ignites my nerves and I let out a squeal. "I wasn't expecting it to be that cold," I whisper to Amber.

Jamie's eyes flatten as he takes a swig of beer. I can feel the heat radiating from his face. How can he possibly be angry with me?

"What's your problem," I whisper.

My boyfriend says nothing, rolls his eyes and chugs the rest of the beer.

"Dude slow your roll," Erik laughs as Jamie tosses the empty beer bottle in the garbage. "The night is still young."

"Yeah, and you drove," I chime in.

"I'm fine," Jamie barks and grabs another beer out of the tub and takes a long and loud gulp. "Unlike some, I know how to handle my alcohol."

What the hell?

26

"Jamie, can I speak with you for a minute...in private?" I ask tugging on his arm.

"Not right now," Jamie says yanking his arm out of my hand. "The party's just getting started."

People start to funnel into the house. Liza, Jeremy and her lackeys, Alison Mayfield, Cameron Links and Heather Friend strut through the foyer followed by the entire lacrosse team. It won't be long before half the school is stumbling through the kitchen.

Liza and her lackeys should be called the "Golden-Haired Triplets." It is amazing how three girls from three different families can be so alike. They have the same holier than thou attitude and according to Liza they are "the Queens of Perkins Harbor." They always dress alike and might as well be one whole bitchy person.

Liza has implemented the rule that they have to color coordinate their outfits based on the day of the week. Seriously. I'm not joking. They shop at Forever 21 because they color coordinate their store. It is the strangest thing and no matter how many times I see them in their matching outfits I think of that Lindsay Lohan movie and with good reason; Liza stole the idea from the movie. On Mondays they wear something black because they hate the first day of the school week and black is meant to signify mourning the weekend. Tuesdays and Wednesdays it is usually some color that begins with the first letter of that specific day so Tuesday they wear turquoise dresses and Wednesday it is watermelon wardrobe day. Cameron tends to take the color names too seriously and actually came to school wearing a dress shaped like a watermelon that she had picked up from the Halloween store at The Mall. Thursdays and Fridays are usually a free-for-all so long as they don't wear any of the colors they've already worn that week and the weekends are their standard, barely there dresses. It's a really confusing system and I'm glad I am not part of their crew.

The new arrivals flock toward the kitchen, well actually they're flocking toward the beer, which just happens to be in the kitchen. Jeremy and Erik fist bump and Alison's date, a scrawny guy with black eyeliner, nods in our direction.

"Hey Erik," Liza says, *sashaying towards us.* "I hear this is supposed to be your best party to date."

Why do I always forget how freaking gorgeous Liza is? It's like she's not even trying to be beautiful, she just is. I'm not sure she really wears any makeup. She probably rolls out of bed and is ready to go looking like a million bucks. It's so not fair. She never has to worry about being made fun of because of a metal halo surrounding her neck. She never has to second guess the decisions she makes because they always work in her favor and she never has to work to get or keep a guy, they will always gravitate to her. But she's a bitch so there's her flaw.

"Hell yeah! This party is going to be off the chains!" Erik shouts into his fist like it's a megaphone.

"Hey Jamie," Liza bats her eyelashes and shifts her hips in his direction.

The sound of his name from her mouth makes me want to hurl. She says it and somehow it oozes sex. Rather than saying, "Let's screw," she would say, "Jamie," and everyone would know that was the signal for sex.

"Liza. I see its Standard Saturday again," Jamie replies.

How the hell does he know about Standard Saturday?

"You know it," Liza does a little spin so everyone can see the skin that she is trying to pass off as a dress. "Oh hey April. I didn't see you there."

Bitch.

"Liza," I reply. "Where's Jeremy? I thought I saw you two come in together."

I slide my arms around Jamie's waist but I might as well be a dog peeing on him to mark my territory.

"Babe!" Jeremy shouts from across the room. I feel like every word he says should be followed by the sound, duuuh. "You have to see this. Michael is chugging two beers at once without any hands!"

I am now replaying *Bill and Ted's Excellent Adventure* in my head. I am sure that if Ted were a real person Jeremy would challenge his level of stupidity. Liza shrugs and rushes over to see this amazing feat that Jeremy's even dumber friend is about to attempt. I really don't understand how those two will be graduating next year.

The kitchen is flooded with people and all I want to do is pull Jamie out of there.

"Jamie, please." I tug on his arm and pull him into the foyer. "What's gotten into you tonight?"

"Nothing. I'm fine," Jamie says. He won't look at me and when he does his eyes dart away so quickly I hardly have time to catch them.

"Okay. I know you. You're not fine. Please tell me what's going on," I plead, caressing his arm.

"I thought I was okay with this but I guess I'm not."

"Okay with what?" I already know what he is talking about.

"The whole Erik thing," he lowers his gaze and stiffens his lower lip. "You had a thing for my best friend."

I knew we shouldn't have come tonight.

"Yes, I *had* a thing for him. That was almost two-years-ago and long before I knew there was a you," I approach him, carefully. I don't want him to pull away when I reach for him. "Jamie, I love you. You're the person I want to be with. Erik means nothing to me and besides if you haven't noticed I'm pretty sure there is something going on between him and Amber."

"Let's just go back to the party," Jamie says and starts for the kitchen.

"Jamie, wait. Talk to me. What can I do to make you feel better about this? You should already know by now that the only person in my heart is you. But if you need more convincing tell me what I need to do and I'll do it. Erik means nothing to me and if I could go back in time and unmeet him I would but since I am not a Time Lord, this is where we are. But I promise you're it. Okay. Shouldn't our marriage conversation on Christmas Eve be a clue that Erik is the furthest thing from my mind? Or the fact that I gave up my virginity to *you*?"

I can almost see the tension weighing on his shoulders. "You should have seen the way you looked at him, April. It was the same way you looked at me that first day we met."

This isn't happening. Jamie can't possibly believe that I would ever look at anyone the way I look at him. I had a crush - a stupid little crush, it is a simple as that.

"Jamie, come on. You can't really believe that."

"It doesn't matter. Let's just go back to the party."

"No! We need to discuss this. I can't believe that after everything and after all this time together you don't trust me."

I have never given him any reason to doubt my feelings for him. I only told him about Erik because I didn't want to hide anything from him. I told him I wanted to marry him for God's sake, what further proof does he need?

"How would you feel if the roles were reversed and I told you that I used to have feelings for Amber?" Jamie asks and waves his hands in the air like he is trying flag down a plane. "Somehow I don't think you'd be singing the same tune right now."

I'll never admit it to him but he has a point. I know I wouldn't be able to handle seeing them together but I also know how little I felt for Erik and how ridiculous it is for Jamie to be holding a former crush against me. Jealousy was never part of his personality. "I don't see a point to being jealous. If we trust one another than that's all that should matter," Jamie had said after meeting Charlie. So either he no longer trusts me or his whole spiel about how pointless jealousy is was a big fat lie.

"I didn't have feelings for Erik! It was a crush a stupid freaking crush and I don't appreciate you using it against me or as a way to embarrass me in front of my friends!"

Jamie loses his balance as though the volume of my voice knocked him over. His shoulders roll and his arms fall at his sides. "And if you want to talk about looking at someone like they're a meal waiting to be eaten, you should have seen your face when Liza walked in."

Shit, why did I say that?

"Don't turn this around on me, April. I've never been interested in Liza!"

"Oh please, you looked at her like she had walked in naked." *Oh my God April, shut the hell up. You're only making things worse.*

"God, April. Just forget it," he says and stomps towards the kitchen that is now swarming with our drunken classmates.

"Are you kidding me? Why do you always walk away?" I shout.

"Because I'd rather not do or say something I am going to regret."

He disappears into the flock of drunken teenagers all of whom shout over the thumping music in inaudible conversation.

My insides are on fire and sweat pools on my neck and back. I want to run after him, to tell him that he is being an idiot and that there is no one else in the world for me, but it's obvious that won't work. I don't know how to fix this. I'm not sure it's actually fixable. I've made things awkward between Jamie and Erik and if it comes down to making a choice between the two of us I know where I'll land. When I was in the 8th grade I had a massive crush on Ryan Jenkins. On Valentine's Day I made Ryan a card with the words, "I like you," painted on the inside. One Friday afternoon Amber got wind of the fact that he was going to ask me to be his girlfriend. I was elated and hauled ass to Ryan's locker where he was already waiting for me. Being the idiotic girl I was, and still am, I threw myself at him and shouted, "I would love to be your girlfriend!" before he even had a chance to open his mouth. That's when I saw the look in his eyes like someone had just killed his favorite pet.

"I can't be your boyfriend April. In fact, I'm not sure we should hang out anymore," Ryan said as he peeled my arms from his neck.

He told me that his best friend, Charlie (yes, *that* Charlie), had a crush on me and made Ryan choose between Charlie and me. He chose his friend. I understood but I was devastated.

And I know that if he has to, Jamie will do the same thing Ryan did. He will chose his best friend over me. If the roles were reversed I would probably do the same for Amber. What's that saying? Lovers come and go but friends are forever?

27

"There you are!" Amber says skipping in from the living room. "I've been looking everywhere for you." Her just-got-done-fooling-around-hair says otherwise. "Are you okay?"

"Well let's see, my world is melting and I'm stuck at this freaking party and all I want to do is go home and eat a tub of mint chocolate chip ice cream" I answer.

I glide toward the stairs and nod to Amber, who follows me upstairs to the first empty room we can find, a bathroom where a porcelain monster came, threw up and then strung up two salmon curtains to cover its tracks.

"Okay what's going on and tell me quickly. I'm afraid if we stay in here too long *we are* going to turn into porcelain," Amber says and slides onto the edge of the bathtub.

The whole conversation with Jamie is playing on repeat in my head. "I thought I was okay with this but I guess I'm not," Jamie's words were as terrifying as him saying, "I don't love you anymore."

"I just had the worst fight with Jamie," my voice cracks.

"Oh geez, about what?" Amber asks as she takes a swig of the blue drink. Vodka and whiskey waft through the air with a sweet and tangy aroma. That wets my palate and I'm tempted to march downstairs and grab a drink myself.

"Erik," I say, flatly.

"Are you serious? Why?" she asks as she chokes on the unfinished sip of alcohol.

"Because he thinks I still have a thing for Erik or something. I don't really know. Trying to get him to talk to me is like pulling teeth."

"Oh God come on dude! You had a small crush on the guy almost two years ago. Besides you're all gaga over Jamie now, sickeningly so. I'm sorry Ape but your man needs to grow up and grow a pair."

"I brought up Liza too and how flirty he was with her before," I say lowering my head and tugging on a loose piece of string that dangles from the curtain.

"April Ruth Marks you did not accuse that boy of having a thing for Liza!" Amber shouts waving her drink around so it mists out of the cup. "What would possess you to do such a thing?"

Whenever either of us has a boy-related issue Amber and I will piece it together like one giant boys-are-impossible puzzle. Usually we do it with a peppermint latte but since those aren't easily accessible I suppose her kitchen-formed-concoction will have to do. I lunge forward and swipe her drink. I take a large swig and the combination of the bitter whiskey and the sweetness of vodka makes my stomach churn.

"I don't know, I panicked."

"Whoa! Slow down. It is far too early for you to be wasted," Amber says and takes back the drink. "Besides you're going to need somewhat of a level head if we're going to sort through this whole Jamie debacle. We have a lot of cleanup to do, especially since you brought up the L-word, and I don't mean love."

Gas rises from the pit of my stomach until it tickles the back of my throat and I release a loud belch. I'd normally be embarrassed but I've done far worse in front of Amber.

"Okay, April that was gross."

"Whatever. Now can we please figure this Jamie thing out?" I ask. I really hope no one was listening because that burp sounded like a school of dying frogs and I have somehow managed to gross myself out.

"Well, he's an idiot for thinking you still have feelings for Erik, but we already knew that."

"Hey, watch it. We might be in a fight right now but I still love the boy."

"I know, I know," Amber takes another swig of her drink and hands it to me. I take another sip and the room begins to spin. "But you're also an idiot for trying to turn the blame around on him."

"Okay, don't let me have anymore. At least not until the room stops moving," I say as moisture begins to soak my face. "How am I going to fix this, Amber? Why did I bring up Liza? He's never shown any interest in her and I know it, I've always known it."

Amber is always joking or making light of every situation but when she needs to be she can be incredibly serious and caring. When my grandma Maggie died Amber was at my house by 9 o'clock every morning for a month. She helped my dad with grocery shopping and doing the laundry, things that my mother and I were too distraught to handle. Even though we were barely teenagers, Amber helped me get through it and I know she'll help me sort through this.

"First, you're not going to lose it while sitting on a toilet in this porcelain hell," Amber says and tosses the now empty glass into the garbage. "Secondly, this is Jamie we're talking about. He's crazy about you, nauseatingly so. The kid can't survive without you. This isn't the end of you guys, not even close. He is going to be mad for a little while, maybe for the rest of the night." I squirm and whimper. Amber slumps off the tub and slides onto her knees in front of me. "But by the end of the night he will realize what an idiot he was being and he will beg for your forgiveness, despite your unwavering stupidity. Besides, he has nothing to worry about. Erik only has eyes for one girl."

This is classic Amber. I already figured out that she and Erik were a thing now but what happened to Alex?

"Seriously, Amber? Like I couldn't see the goo-goo eyes you two were throwing at each other earlier," I say patting her head. "When did all of this happen and what about Alex? I thought you were really falling for him?"

Amber melts to the floor and throws her hand onto her forehead. "I don't know how it happened, Ape," she whines. "I was falling for Alex but then last week when my car broke down Erik happened to drive by and waited with me until the mechanic came and I don't know, we got to talking and," Amber slaps the floor and slithers around like a worm. "He is so much more than the dumb jock everyone thinks he is. He's deep and sexy and ugh he makes me feel alive, you know?"

She used to call him, "Doctor Stinky Pants," when we were in Kindergarten. She disliked him to the point where when I had my crush on him she'd say things like, "You don't want Erik. I hear he's got some irreversible disease." It is eerie to hear her calling Erik "sexy" and what's more she's calling him, "deep." I might have had a crush on Erik but even I know he isn't *deep*.

"So I take it he's been cleared of all disease then," I tease. "Seriously though, what happened with Alex?"

"He is such a good guy and he treated me the way any girl wants a guy to. I don't know, when everything started with Erik, all the excitement I felt when I was with Alex disappeared. I feel terrible but wouldn't it have been worse if I lead him on and continued to see Erik behind his back?"

Wow. With every breakup she's ever had I am usually the first person to find out. Since Jamie and I got serious, Amber and I haven't really been as close. We used to hang out every day and talk on the phone at least five times a day when we weren't together, especially when her mother would pull her out of school for some new adventure. But lately we're lucky if we talk on the phone more than once and when we do it's usually a five minute conversation about how annoying school is. We don't talk the way we used to.

"Hey Amber," I stammer. Having deep conversations about our friendship has never been our strong suit, boys sure - but us - not as easy. "Why didn't you tell me about Alex or Erik when it happened?"

"I tried, Ape but you were so wrapped up in your 6-month anniversary dinner," Amber replies.

I am both the worst friend and girlfriend ever. "Amber, I'm really sorry I've been such a shitty friend lately."

I have more to say but she throws a clammy hand up to shut me up. "No, no, no. We're at a high school party, being thrown by the guy I happen to be hooking up with. We've already had our Lifetime movie moment and I'm too tipsy to have anymore."

"No, but I feel really bad. You know you can always talk to me, right?"

"Oh geez, yes Ape I know. Stop being so dramatic. Now, if you're not melting anymore, can we please go back to the party?

28

The house is roaring with conversations going at once and every room is crawling with kids from school; it is louder than sitting front row at a Backstreet Boys concert, not that I know what that sounds like…yet. Amber and I make our way into the kitchen.

"I know Eric said this party was going to be huge but this is ridiculous!" I yell. Less than an hour ago this house was enormous now it's like standing in a powder room.

"Do you see Jamie anywhere?" I shout over the clamor of drunk teens.

She peeks around the crowd that is barricading the entrance to the kitchen, "No. All I see is too much gel and a lot of bad dye jobs."

"Amber!" Erik calls from the middle of the teenage mosh pit.

I can't see him but I see a beer bottle floating towards us. A patch opens enough for me to see a section of the kitchen but I don't see Jamie. It is going to be hard to pick him out of this crowd of blue denim jeans and skirts so short they leave little to the imagination.

"Geez, did you invite the entire town to this thing?" Amber says as Erik reaches us and hands her a beer.

"It seems that way doesn't it?" Erik replies and hustles us out of the kitchen and back into the foyer. "Whew. I really wasn't expecting this many people. I mean I knew this party was going to be crazy but this is out of control. This must be Liza's doing. She always had a big mouth."

He would know. During our freshman year Erik and Liza dated for a few weeks. Well, actually they weren't officially dating so much as they were hooking up. Liza is the first of the girls my age that I know of, to lose her virginity. She has always been a free spirit for lack of a kinder word. After they broke up or stopped screwing Liza and Erik had a massive blowout in the middle of the cafeteria but he still continues to invite her to these parties. I'm not really sure why.

"Erik! Bitchin party!" Michael shouts and waves his beer back and forth. It spills all over him. "Shit. This is a brand new shirt!" Amazing how all that stupid can fit into one person.

I roll my eyes, which Erik notices and shoves me playfully.

"He may be dumb but Michael is a freak of nature on the lacrosse field."

Girls choose their friends based on the quality of their personality and their loyalty whereas boys choose their friends based on their level of talent on the sports field.

"Hey, where's Jamie?" I ask.

In my head Jamie is sitting in the middle of a cluster of people so drunk they can hardly hold themselves upright. People are probably bumping into him and girls throw their drunken bodies at him but he's ignoring it all. He's feeling as badly as I feel and is trying to look for me too.

Erik bites his bottom lip and rubs my shoulder softly. "I'm so sorry, April but Jamie left."

"What?" Amber shouts so loudly that a group of boys standing by the front door turn to look at us. "What do you mean he left? He's our freaking ride home. His girlfriend is here! How could he just freaking leave?"

This is it. This is the moment I've been dreading since Jamie first kissed me on the Ocean Walk all those months ago. I know this isn't a Hollywood romance but I had hoped we would be the ones to last. How can you say you want to marry someone and then let something as stupid as a fight turn everything upside-down? I think I've been preparing for this for the last six months. I feel sick and the liquor and beer are not sitting well. I need to get out of here.

"Don't worry, I'll give you a ride home," Erik says, placing his drink on the stairs.

"Did he say why?" I whisper trying to force the bubble in my throat back down.

"Why?"

"He left? Did he say why he left?"

I already know.

"Not really, no. He just said he had something he needed to do."

Yeah, he had to ditch me at a party because he's too afraid to face me and break up with me in person. Turns out he's not perfect after all.

"Erik, do you think you can take me home now I'm not feeling very well."

"I'll get your stuff," Erik says and grabs my shirt and purse out of the closet.

Amber grabs her purse and heads for the door but she came here to be with Erik and just because I'm heartbroken doesn't mean she has to be miserable with me.

"You don't have to leave if you don't want to," I say to Amber as she wraps her arm around my shoulder. She cocks an eyebrow at me and her lips flatten. "Really, I'll be okay. Stay. It's fine."

"You sure?" I nod.

"I'm sure. Stay. I'll be okay."

"Promise?"

"I promise," this is the first time I have ever lied to her.

"Okay, but I'm there if you need me to be," Amber pulls me in. "Whatever you need."

"Ready to go?" Erik says as he twirls his keys around his finger.

"She's staying," I nod in Amber's direction.

Why should they be upset just because I am? They are in the honeymoon phase of their relationship and if anyone knows how wonderful that can be it's me. I guess that's over now.

29

Erik's Hummer spits as we pull up to my house. Normally I don't like coming home to an empty house but I'm grateful for the quiet. I'm not in a talking mood and if I pretended to be okay my parents would see right through the act and I'd be up all night explaining the fight to them.

"Doesn't look like anyone is home," Erik says as he leans forward to look out my window. If this were two-years-ago I would be a frantic mess having his face this close to me. I feel like those days are from another lifetime.

The exterior of the house is unsettlingly dark. Most nights, when they go out or if I am getting home after they've gone to bed, my parents will leave the porch light on so I don't stumble up the stairs but Dad broke it last week when he was battling a spider.

"My parents and Amber's are out tonight," I reply.

"Maybe I should bring you back to the party. You can hang out in my room, watch a movie or whatever at least until someone comes home. Or we can swing back to my house and pick Amber up and she can stay with you until your parents come home."

It's not that Erik has never been caring toward others before, during the summer he volunteers at York's Assisted Living Facility, but he's always been this goofy jock who says things like, "Dude!" and "Off the hook." I've never seen this side of him before.

"Thanks, but I'll be okay,"

"Hey so I heard you're writing a book. Is that true?" Erik asks.

My family, Amber and Jamie are the only people who know about my recreational habits so Jamie must have told him.

"I'm trying to but it's not as easy as I thought it would be," I say.

"Well, it's pretty awesome that you're trying though. Jamie was super proud of you when he told me about it."

The distance in Jamie's eyes as we stood in Erik's foyer tonight and the uncertainty of where our relationship lies stings as I remember promising Jamie that he would be the first person to read my book. I can't believe how far we've fallen in the last hour.

"Did he say anything? Jamie, before he left? Other than that he had something to do?"

"Look," Erik puts his hand on my knee the way my father does when he is trying to comfort me. "I don't know what happened between you two but just give him time. He'll come around."

Isn't it strange that the person who is the cause of the fight is the one trying to reassure me?

"Yeah. Maybe. Thanks for the ride." I say as I pull the lock on the door. I can't remember the last time I was in a car with manual locks.

"Hey, April," Erik flips his head to remove the hair from his forehead. "I'm sorry about what you've had to go through this year. You know with the master lock incident and everything."

I didn't think anyone, except Jamie, my parents and Amber knew about that. I didn't want anyone else knowing about it because I knew they would do one of two things, they would either make fun of me for it or give me the sympathetic puppy-dog-eyed look Erik is giving me right now. "You know I would have gladly kicked their asses for you."

"I know," I laugh. "How did you hear about that?" I ask, picking at the red nail polish that has begun to chip on my fingers. "Were kids talking about it at school? I have seen people whispering a lot more than usual when I walk by them in the halls."

"No, Jamie told me," Erik says, cocking his head to the side.

He is just spilling everything about me isn't he?

"He did? Why?" I can feel the heat rising to my cheeks.

"He came over a few days after it happened and he was in such a bad mood and seemed so angry. I prodded him until he told me. He said it took every ounce of strength he had not to find those guys and kick their asses."

I knew he was angry but I had no idea Jamie was still bothered by the incident days later. He might have been a jerk tonight, but what kind of a girlfriend would I be if this didn't make me smile a little bit?

"Yeah he was pretty angry about it."

"So whatever happened between you two tonight, do the kid a favor and cut him some slack. Dude, he's crazy in love with you."

"Thanks Erik, I appreciate that."

"One last thing and then I promise I'm done counseling you," Erik teases. "No matter what idiots say, you're still awesome with or without that brace."

I stumble backward and catch myself on the door handle. This isn't Erik Marshall, school jock I am looking at, it's Erik Marshall, my friend.

"Thank you, Erik. That really means a lot," I reply. "I'll be okay though, I have Jamie."
Do I still have Jamie?

The house is eerily quiet. I've been home alone before but usually my dad's mother, Grandma Alison, comes to stay with me but she's still getting over the flu. While I could really use one of her delicious cherry pies, I welcome the quiet. If she were here she would ask me a million questions about Jamie and I'd have to either lie to her or tell her about the fight. Grandma Alison is great at giving advice but I'd rather not listen to advice. Right now, I want to open a tub of ice cream and drown myself in sugar and the Backstreet Boys.

Our fridge is like a who's who of small farm foods. Mom and dad do most of their shopping at the local market, Maine's Best a small grocery store in town. We have things like Maine's Best Milk, Maine's Best Water, Maine's Best Apples and you get the picture, most of their products come from farms and small town factories. So instead of Breyer's I pull out a carton of Maine's Best Mint Chocolate Chip. It basically tastes the same as Breyer's but for the ice cream experts, like Amber who always has to have Breyer's, it has a cardboard flavor to it. I don't taste the difference but even if I did it will do the trick.

I fluff up the pillows on the couch, including the one with a black patch on it that my mother tried to sew in an attempt to be more domestic, and pop in *Backstreet Boys: In Concert* circa 1998 and throw open the ice cream. I'm ready to wallow and allow the soulful sounds and smooth dance moves of the boys to take me to a happy place. The video gears up and the roaring sound of the screaming crowd floods my living room. It takes me back to the second time I saw them live.

I had dragged Amber, practically kicking and screaming, to the State Theatre in Portland because I had no one else to go with. The venue wasn't anything spectacular and seemed rather small for the thousands of teenage girls flooding the double doors to get inside. I felt like we were about to walk into a different dimension where only teenage girls and the five men in the group existed, and that would have been fine with me. The moment my foot hit the pavement in front of the venue I was running on adrenaline. I didn't care that we had nosebleed seats. I didn't care that a fellow Backstreet Boys fan had spilled her soda on me when we collided whilst running to find our seats. I didn't care that Charlie had called me ten times in under an hour. All I cared about was the fact that we were there in the same building as my idols. As the lights dimmed and the crowd erupted, I looked over at Amber hoping that she was at least slightly excited, but she was just sitting there with a blank look on her face. The entire crowd was on its feet screaming and jumping up and down and my best friend was playing Temple Run on her phone. I should have been annoyed because I had paid for the tickets with my allowance and because who doesn't scream and freak out at a Backstreet Boys concert? But I had no room for annoyance because all I could feel was euphoria as my boys exploded on stage.

They were magnetic and pulled the loudest and most uncontrollable screams out of me. I felt like my throat would fall out. For the two hours the group was onstage I thought about nothing other than the sheer joy of seeing those boys live. All of the stress that went along with being a freshman in high school, the worry about how unhappy I was with Charlie, wearing the back brace and anything else that might have plagued me that day, fell away like ash burning in a fire. Those five men were there for me no matter what mood I was in and seeing them, no matter how small they looked, only increased my respect for them. There was nothing like hearing their voices serenading the crowd and giving us all they had. I remember being so grateful to them for so much and not just giving me an escape from my problems, but for giving me hope in times when I didn't think there was any.

I had written them a letter a long time ago thanking them for changing my life but, as most fan mail does, I am sure it was tossed in with the millions of other thank you notes, teddy bears, drawings and underwear (not mine…ever) that they receive on a daily basis. Still, I fantasize that one day I'll receive a letter from them or some kind of acknowledgement. What can I say? I'm optimistic, sometimes.

That night in Portland was the happiest I had ever been until Mrs. Honor's class six-months-ago when Jamie asked me to be his girlfriend. Isn't it amazing how things can change so quickly? A few hours ago Jamie and I were happy, in-love and feeling like we could take on the world and now I'm sitting here eating a carton of ice cream, watching the same video I've watched a hundred times and I'm completely shattered. Maybe I should just call him and ask him to come over so we can work this through. But he *left* me at that party. So *he* should be the one to call *me*!

I have to be strong and I have to, "make him grovel," that's what Amber had said before Erik took me home. "You make him beg for your forgiveness and if he calls or texts you tonight don't jump on your phone, let him wait it out." She was very insistent about it and usually when she's that clear on her instructions she knows what she is talking about.

I slink onto my back and fluff the throw pillows so they're comfortable enough to lie on and focus on the music. I hope the boys do what they've always done for me and take me away from the thoughts in my head.

30

Buzz, buzz, buzz. The vibration of the phone bouncing around on the coffee table wakes me up. I didn't even realize I fell asleep. I catch the phone mid-bounce and pull it to my face. I rub my eyes and try reading the name on the screen again. JAMIE CALLING. Ha! Ha! Amber was right he really couldn't go an entire night without speaking to me. Part of me wants to answer it and apologize for everything but the other part of me wants to let it go to voicemail.

"I can't believe you used my being honest about the whole Erik thing as ammunition in a fight!" I shout at the vibrating phone. Ugh!

Buzz, buzz, buzz. JAMIE CALLING. No! I didn't have to tell him about the Erik thing because it is irrelevant but I didn't want to hide things from him but if this is how it is going to be every time I tell him something he might not like we're going to have serious problems.

"Jamie, don't say anything," I say as I pick up the incessantly buzzing phone. "I'm really hurt and pissed off at how you treated me tonight. I told you the truth about Erik because I didn't want to hide anything from you and you turned it around on me! That's not okay!"

"I know," he replies. His voice is low and quiet.

"Where are you?" I ask as I listen to the chattering voices of a crowd on the other end of the line.

A high squeaky voices jumps through the phone and heat surges through me as I recognize Liza's voice and hear the baritone sound Erik makes when he laughs. He's still there! Jamie never left the party! UN-FREAKING-BELIEVABLE! I slump onto the floor with my legs rolled against me.

"Are you kidding me?" I shout. I could scream and throw up all at the same time. "You know what Jamie, you walked away earlier because you didn't want to say something you'd regret, well now it's my turn!" CLICK.

I slam the phone on the coffee table and the screen cracks. "Shit!"

I cannot believe Jamie did this. I've learned that Jamie is not perfect but I never expected *this*. I would never ditch him at a party and I sure as hell wouldn't lie about it. We've never lied to one another. My heart is thumping wildly and flashes of cold burrow through my spine until they shoot out from my toes. The ceiling and walls are closing in and every breath I take is a struggle. I need my best friend.

Buzz, buzz, buzz. I almost don't want to look. *Buzz, buzz, buzz.* I should ignore it but I swear my cell phone is like this giant magnet that pulls me in every time. Still on the floor, I swipe the phone off the table and brace myself. AMBER CALLING.

"You have the best timing," I sing.

"Jamie is still here," Amber whispers. "He's such a dick!"

"Yeah, I know. He called me right before you did and I heard Erik and that bitch Liza in the background. I swear every time I hear her ugly-ass voice I want to punch something. I know she is trying to get with Jamie. She thinks I can't see it but I can."

Okay, maybe I am focusing on the wrong issue but I know what my gut is telling me; Liza has her eye on Jamie. This is what she does. Why do girls like Liza exist? Shouldn't they be reserved for soap operas or romantic comedies? She's not really that pretty. Okay, fine so she's pretty but so is Jennifer Aniston and you don't see her trying to steal other people's boyfriends.

"Ape? April? Hello?" Amber shouts as she seems to be shoving the entire phone in her mouth. Her voice snaps me back from my 'I hate Liza trance.'

"Yes, I'm here you don't have to yell," I snap pretending like I didn't miss the last minute of whatever it was she was saying. "Amber, did he say anything to you? You know, about our fight and me? Or about the fact that he is a total dick nugget for pretending to ditch me at the party?"

"No, but he is pretty much avoiding me and that's smart. I told you if he ever hurt you it would be the last thing he ever did."

Actually her exact words were, "The minute he makes you cry I am going to take him to Camp Pain and by the time I'm done with him not only will he be celibate he'll never look at another girl again."

"I can't believe he did this. It makes no sense. Why pretend to be okay with something that took place two-years-ago if you're not? Why be mad about something that is so irrelevant? Why are boys so freaking confusing?"

"There's no point in trying to make sense of Jamie's stupidity. He's a boy, which means stupid is embedded in him and it was only a matter of time before it reared its ugly head," Amber snorts.

Whenever she says something she thinks is really clever she'll snort while she is laughing and right now she sounds more like a Potbelly than my best friend.

"Amber," I say flatly.

"Sorry, sorry. So I know you're probably sitting on your couch downing an entire carton of ice cream and watching one of your bazillion Backstreet Boys DVDs, yuck, but as soon as Erik is done kicking Jeremy out because he puked in Mrs. Marshall's favorite vase, he is going to drop me at your house," Amber explains.

"No, you don't have to do that," I protest, weakly.

"Ape, there's no need to pretend. I know you're wallowing and what kind of friend would I be if I let you wallow alone?"

After the call from Jamie I swore I was done crying for the night...so much for that.

"Okay," *sniffle, sob, snot,* "thank you, Amber," *sniffle, sob, snot* "I'll see you soon."

Amber sighs and muffles her voice, "Erik, we gotta go...now!"

I wonder how Marlo would handle a situation like this. I doubt she'd be sitting in the dark crying about a boy. Unlike me, she doesn't need anyone else to give her self-worth. I wish I were more like her then maybe I wouldn't feel this shitty right now. I'd also be invisible.

31

I throw my arms around Amber's neck as she hangs her jacket on the coat rack in the foyer. It took her less than ten minutes to get here but in those ten minutes I finished the rest of the ice cream, had two pieces of the chocolate cake and destroyed the plate of rainbow cookies Mrs. Hill made for the family. Had Amber not come tonight I probably would have finished all the junk food in the cabinets as well.

"Has he called you again?" Amber asks.

Jamie's face enters my mind. I know I told him to give me space but the truth is, I don't want space I just want Jamie.

"No, I told him not to," I reply and flop beside her on the couch. "Did you see him before you left?"

Amber shifts against the arm of the couch and fluffs the pillow that I had cried and screamed into earlier. She picks up the carton of ice cream and pokes at it with her finger. She manages to scrape a few licks of ice cream from the sides of the carton and tosses it in the air towards the waste basket. It floats and lands inches from the pail. I've noticed something; whenever Jamie sends garbage flying toward the pail it always goes in but if Amber or I try somehow it ends up landing just short of the garbage. What is that about?

"So," I say, "did you see Jamie before you left?"

"I did. He didn't say anything to me though."

"No, I figured he wouldn't." I pick up a pillow and braid pieces of yarn that dangle off the edges of it. "Was he with Liza?"

Amber rolls her eyes and slides so her feet dangle enough to reach the coffee table.

"I don't agree with how Jamie acted tonight and I think he's a freaking moron for using the whole Erik thing against you but you have got to get over this Liza thing. He's never shown any interest in her and every time she's tried to make a move he's either ignored it or turned her away."

"She's made a move on him before?" I launch off the couch and stand with my arms folded. "How? When?" I demand as my shoulders begin to involuntarily twitch.

I knew she had her eyes on him but I didn't realize she's actually tried to take him from me. When did this happen? How did I not know about it? Why didn't he tell me about it? Okay, I know *why* he didn't tell me but still, isn't this the kind of thing I should know about?

"Dude. Relax," says Amber. "As I said it didn't work. I swear, if I didn't know you better I'd think you had a thing for Liza with how much you obsess over her."

"Oh come on. She's a sneaky bitch. If she were going after Erik again you'd be saying the same thing."

"Yeah. Well. Still you really need to give it a rest. Jamie is so not interested in her. He's too goo-goo eyed for you."

Full disclosure, I love hearing how gaga for me Jamie is. If outsiders can see it then it must be true.

With me off the couch, Amber takes advantage of the room and stretches out her legs across and rests her hands behind her head. She stares at the ceiling smiling but my mundane ceiling isn't why she has that euphoric grin that I had every time I thought about

Jamie over the last six-months or those same wide cat eyes. I know she's thinking about Erik.

"Hey, got any peppermint?" Amber asks and she jolts up.

"Of course we do!"

It's amazing how bubbly the idea of peppermint coffee can make me. Tonight the excitement over the coffee is because I know that by the time the cups are empty Amber and I will have determined if I should call Jamie.

"Do you think Jamie and I will get past this?" I ask once we've had a few sips of the coffee.

I have been sitting on that question for the last hour. I wanted to ask Amber the minute she walked in but I've been too afraid. She is usually brutally honest, which I appreciate, but sometimes hearing it sucks. I cross my fingers under the table and wait for her response.

"Ape, come on. It's you and Jamie, of course you will." she says, taking another sip of coffee. "This is just a small hump in your sickeningly perfect romance"

The 6-ton elephant that had been sitting on my chest since Amber came over jumps off and breathing becomes easier. But to be safe...

"What makes you so sure?"

Buzz, buzz, buzz. I hear a muffled vibration coming from the other room. I must have left my phone in the living room! No wonder I felt so naked. I almost never go anywhere without it.

Buzz, buzz, buzz. I throw the chair back and jump to my feet and rush to grab my phone.

"No!" Amber roars. "Sit back down."

I pause and turn to face her. "Umm...why?" She gulps the last few sips of coffee and places the cup down. She looks at me the way my mother does when she's about to lay down some generational advice. But Amber says nothing, she just stares blankly at me. We're super close but I am no mind reader so this whole Jedi-mind-trick thing isn't going to work. "Hello? Earth to Amber! Why can't I get my phone?"

Buzz, buzz, buzz.

"Okay this is ridiculous! I can't stand here and have a staring contest with you while my phone is taunting me!" I race into the living room and snatch the phone off the table. TWO MISSED CALLS: JAMIE. "Lovely!" I click back to the home screen and search for Jamie's number in my favorites list.

"Seriously?" Amber shouts as she waltzes towards me. She shakes her head and buries her face in the palm of her hand.

"I'm not like you, Amber," I whine and throw my hands on my hips. "I can't just let things roll off my shoulders. Life isn't always glass half-full."

I tried not to let Jamie become my life, I really did but he broke every wall I had down and eventually I had no choice but to give in.

"You don't have to be glass-half full to know when to stand your ground, Ape," says Amber as she allows her arms to fall at her sides.

"This is the second time he's called me in the last hour, look two missed calls," I say shoving the phone in her face.

"April, the guy started a fight with you in the middle of a high school party, he used your honesty with him against you and he freaking lied to you! Do I really need to tell you why you should continue to freeze him out…at least for a little while longer?" she begs, clapping her hands together.

All I want to do right now is pick up my phone and call Jamie back. I want to hear the sound of his voice and feel the safety of knowing he loves me. I want to rewind the last two nights and take back everything I told him about Erik. Unfortunately I can only live in the here and now but that doesn't mean I am going to be happy about it.

"Damn you, Amber," I scoff but relent. "I'll let him sweat it out. But as punishment we're going upstairs and I'm making you listen to the new Backstreet Boys album cover-to-cover."

She just won a battle so she doesn't argue and follows me upstairs, albeit she is walking pretty slowly. Procrastination won't save her tonight.

32

You know those dreams that feel so real that when you wake up and open your eyes you're not sure if you're still inside the dream? Well, right now I can't figure out if all the eyes staring at me are coming from the posters on my ceiling or if I'm still dreaming. I hope I'm awake. The dream I was having is not one I want to live in. I dreamt about Jamie, big surprise right? But this wasn't one of those fantastic dreams where we're running through some flower field in slow motion. It was a nightmare.

We were standing in a tiny room; well, it was more like a door less alabaster closet with a ceiling that forced Jamie to hunch over so his head wouldn't smash through it. We were engulfed in a musty smell - like mothballs and dirt. I couldn't breathe and as panic began to set in I looked to Jamie for help but he just stood there, staring right through me like he wasn't even really there, as if his body were just a shell. I tried to get him back, to snap his soul back into his body. I shook him, screamed at him, "Jamie! Jamie! Talk to me. Jamie, come back to me!" Nothing worked, every time I tried the walls slid closer and closer together. I knew that the room was going to crush us if we didn't get out but there was nowhere to go. There was nothing but wall. I threw my weight onto the wall closest to us and pushed with everything I had to try to get it to stop moving but nothing worked.

My feet began to slip from under me and when I looked for him, Jamie was gone. I screamed for him but my screams seemed to move the walls closer to me more quickly. As darkness consumed me I screamed one final time for Jamie.

So here I am sweating, disoriented and half off the bed. Amber takes up as much room on the bed as a 500-pound man. My heart is racing and I try to rub the sleep from my eyes but the daze of the dream still hasn't worn off. I flip onto my back and stare at the poster of the Backstreet Boys on my ceiling. Five familiar faces smile at me. I rub the corner of the blanket where the seams were sewn together. It feels real and I can hear crickets singing outside and the hum of the dehumidifier that I've used every night since I was a baby, so I must be awake.

I have always been fascinated with the concept of dream interpretation and have read dozens of books on the subject so I can analyze the dream, but the interpretation for dreaming about a room without any windows and doors is about pregnancy and the womb. Jamie and I have only ever had sex once and that was a few weeks ago and we were safe, so I know I am not pregnant. It has to be something else. Besides the shrinking room isn't what is making me feel uneasy right now, it's the Jamie shell. Maybe my dream is trying to show me what I'm afraid of, that after tonight Jamie's feelings for me have changed. But that doesn't make any sense either. You don't fall out of love with someone just because you have a fight, right? Maybe I should wake up Amber and ask her what she thinks but she hates being woken up and lets me know it. When we were little and would have sleepovers I would make the mistake of waking her up in the middle of the night. She'd scream about how horrible of a friend I was and then she'd spend the next ten minutes tossing on, kicking and punching the bed. You would think I would have learned after the first few times but I didn't and continued to wake her until we were in our teens. Once you reach a certain size the violence against the bed changes and turns on you, the best friend.

Buzz. My phone bounces around the nightstand and stops abruptly. I pull the phone off the charger read the screen. NEW VOICEMAIL.

Hey April its Jamie. The ache in his voice makes my stomach turn. *I've been sitting on the beach staring at the waves for the last two-hours trying to figure out what to say to you. I thought about coming over but after we spoke and when you didn't answer your phone I figured you meant it when you said you needed space. I get it.* He sighs and breathes heavily for a few seconds. *I can't tell you how sorry I am about how I acted tonight. I don't know what came over me. I saw Erik and you and I don't know I snapped. I guess seeing you two together, okay I know you weren't together but you know what I mean, just struck a nerve. I know lying about ditching you was the worst thing I could have done and if I could go back and change it I would. I'm not sure if you can but I really hope you will forgive me. I think I just got afraid because I know you're it for me. I'm done looking for the one because I have found her and that freaks me out a little bit. But I also think that's a good thing.*

Anyway, I just had to call and tell you how sorry I am. I'll be up for

a while so you can call me if you want. If not I'll try again

tomorrow. I love you, April.

I click the home button to check the time. 1:03 a.m. It is too late to call him tonight but its okay because I will call him first thing in the morning.

33

"April, sweetie. Wake up," mom says, and gently brushes her hand against my cheek.

Her voice is shaky and broken. The last time she sounded like this was when she told me that Grandmother Maggie died. I open my eyes and see mom kneeling in front of me. Sleep hasn't receded from her eyes yet and her lips are cracked and blistered.

"Anna, is she awake?" my father says quietly as he enters the room and joins her at my bedside. He mirrors the worn out look my mother is wearing. "Hi sweetie."

"Ape, you awake?" Amber says softly.

I feel the mattress dip as Amber climbs onto the bed and sits beside me. She's sniffling and coughs like she's got something stuck in her throat. Why is she so upset? Why is everyone else in this room acting like *the* world is about to implode? Amber places her hand on my shoulder and I can feel the weight of her sadness pushing on my lungs. My head is heavy, spinning and I feel sick to my stomach. My mother and father's eyes are dripping as they glide to their feet and clutch one another and stare at me a little too long. I feel small the way I used to feel when I was younger and would get in trouble. I am sick of looking at their sad faces and tired of them staring at me just waiting for me to fall apart.

On my phone I have ten missed calls from Mrs. Clarke and six voicemails, which are probably from Jamie's mom. Six voicemails, six messages telling me every word I've never wanted to hear. Everyone here knows about those messages but there's one that only *I* know about. *I know you're it for me. I'm done looking for the one because I have found her.* When the words stop and silence returns I know what has happened. No one has to say it. I already know. Jamie is gone.

34

For the last forty-eight-hours I have been going through the motions and doing all of the things a girl should do after her boyfriend dies. I have made the appropriate phone calls for his parents to their family and friends. I have locked myself in my room for hours and listened to all the songs that remind me of Jamie. I have said the appropriate things like, "I loved him so much," and "I'm so lucky to have been loved by him." I've helped Mr. and Mrs. Clarke make funeral arrangements and even helped Jamie's mom pick out the casket he would be buried in. I have done everything I am supposed to do in this kind of situation. But I haven't felt the weight of it. I don't deserve to.

The funeral is set for 10 o'clock a.m. at the Perkins Harbor funeral home, where most people in this town go to say goodbye. I have less than an hour before I have to face a room full of Jamie's loved ones who will see me as the girl Jamie wanted to spend the rest of his life with. The girl he *did* spend the rest of his life with.

The *one*. They won't see the person I see when I look in the mirror, the girl responsible for Jamie's death.

"April, how are you doing?" mom asks, poking her head in the room. She's already dressed. Her hair, that has sprouted a few new grey patches over the last two days, is pulled back and held together with one of Grandma Maggie's butterfly clips.

"It won't stay," I say and toss my hair in a clump on top of my head. My fingers are wet and sticky and covered in broken pieces of hair from the last hour of yanking. "I keep trying but it just keeps breaking."

Mom glides in, grabs the mass of hair and twists, pulls and flips it until it is latched up with a hair tie. She places her hands on my shoulders and stares at me through our reflection in the mirror. "You're strong April, you'll get through this."

I smile and touch her hands with mine. "No I won't," I whisper.

"I know it doesn't seem like it now sweetie but you will, I promise," she says and smiles widely but her eyes remain lowered and empty.

"You shouldn't make promises you can't keep, mom."

She stands next to me and grabs my hands and forces me to look at her. She has that motherly look in her eyes like she thinks her advice will change anything. You know that look when her eyes get wider and her lips flatten right before she speaks? I think all parents have that all-knowing look and this is hers.

"April Rose Marks, you listen to me. You will get through this. You will come out on the other side because you are strong and have so much in life to look forward to."

"No mom, I don't. Two days ago I did because I had Jamie. Now, I have nothing but this pain in my chest and aching in my stomach," I say. "Unless you're talking about the fact that I can be held accountable for his death."

I shouldn't have said anything. Why have I not learned my lesson about what I should and should not admit to my parents? I didn't tell her when I realized that Jamie was the one so why did I tell her *this*?

"Mom?" I ask hesitantly. I don't really want to get into this right now but it's awkward with her sitting here staring at me like I'm the one who died.

"How can you say such a thing?" Mom says after many seconds of silence.

"Because it's the truth."

"Why? How? Please, make me understand."

She knows why. After Jamie died I explained it all to her. I told her about the fight and the phone calls. I let her hear his voicemail and she knew that I had made the decision not to call him and to let my pride control my choices. She knew that he was at the beach waiting for me to call him back and that he went into the waves because that's what *we* did on our first date and that's why he was pulled under by the current. So why is she asking me to make her understand? Shouldn't she already get it?

"You know why," I insist and slide into the navy blue skirt and grey blouse that I had determined would be my Jamie's funeral dress.

Today is going to be hard enough and even though I didn't ask their permission I determined that I would not be wearing the brace today. I don't want my last time seeing Jamie to be with that cage on me. I look smaller without it on. This is how I will look the last time I ever see Jamie. Funny, this isn't how I pictured it. I thought I would have a lot more wrinkles, would be covered in silver hair and be horizontal and hooked up to a bunch of machines and wires. I thought I'd see him sitting beside me, holding my hand and telling me how happy our lives together had made him. Isn't it amazing how you can plan things out so carefully and just like that everything changes?

"April, you listen to me and listen well. Did you physically put Jamie on the beach that night? Did you force him into the water, force the waves to grab him and pull him under?

I know what she is doing but it isn't going to work. I might not have been the one who ended Jamie's life that night but had I answered my phone I could have convinced Jamie to come over and he wouldn't have been anywhere near the beach. He would still be alive. I have made many mistakes in my life but this is the worst. This one I'll live with the rest of my life.

"No, of course I didn't," I reply. "But that doesn't mean I'm not responsible, mom."

She opens her mouth but dad is calling her from downstairs. "Anna, can you come down here for a minute?"

"In a minute," mom shouts and rolls her eyes.

"Anna, Mrs. Clarke is on the phone for you," dad insists.

Mom sighs and lifts herself off the bed and pats me on the arm. "I *have* to take this but you have to stop blaming yourself for this, April. You did everything right with him. You loved him through and through and he knew it. Everyone did. Nothing you could have done differently would have changed what happened that night. The universe has a plan and this was its plan for Jamie and you can't fight it but you also can't blame yourself."

I smile and nod not because I agree with her but because if I don't pretend to she'll never leave and right now Jamie's mom needs her more than I do. She kisses me on the cheek and heads downstairs to take Mrs. Clarke's phone call. When Jamie was alive, my parents never spent much time with the Clarkes. But the last couple of day's

mom and Mrs. Clarke have been speaking on the phone every couple

of hours. It's weird how tragedy can pull people together like that.

Not that Jamie and I needed our parents to be "besties" or anything

but it would have been nice had their friendship developed for a

better reason.

Knock, knock, knock. Amber wraps on the door lightly.

"Ape?"

I didn't know she was coming over before the funeral. I

assumed I'd meet her there but I'm not surprised to see her.

"I'm decent you can come in," I say, without thinking.

I have lived in this room for the last 17-years of my life and

Amber has been in here every day for almost as long but as she

walks toward me I feel like I'm standing in an unfamiliar place.

Nothing looks the way it is supposed to. The friendly faces that

cover my walls and ceiling look at me with judgmental eyes. They

know what I did.

"You look nice," she says and hugs me. The chain of her necklace snags in my hair. "Oh shoot, sorry." She tugs at it until the caught strands of hair break off.

I shrug. My hair breaking is something I've become used to lately.

On most of the people that I know, a black funeral dress makes them look elderly and depressing. On Amber it looks like she has stepped out of an Old Navy catalogue. We always used to joke about moving to New York so she could become a runway model like Kate Moss but when she and Johnny Depp broke up Amber's interest in the modeling industry died out. With Jamie gone the idea of getting out of Perkins Harbor and into a big city is pretty tempting.

"So," Amber asks "Are you okay? I don't mean the kind of okay where you pretend that you're strong and not suffering, I mean the real kind of okay."

"Would you be?"

There is only one answer. It is impossible to be okay when something this horrible happens. After this you know that you're never going to be okay again.

"Ape," Amber twirls her hair through her fingers and I can see them shaking. "I'm so sorry," she sobs. "I wouldn't let you call him. It wasn't my place. I wouldn't let you call him. I should have let you call him. I'm so sorry" am so, so sorry."

"You didn't do anything wrong, Amber. I had all night to call him back and swallow my pride but *I* choose not to. This is *my* fault, not yours. I don't blame you."
I grab Amber and as we cry together we hold onto each other tightly.

"Can I ask you something else then," once again Amber lowers her gaze and bites the tips of her fingernails. "I'm not trying to upset you or make it harder for you but…" her voice trails off. "Do you regret it?"

"Regret what?"

"Jamie. Do you regret meeting him and falling in love with him now that he's gone?"

I've asked myself this question at least a hundred times. It would be so easy to say yes because had Jamie and I never met I wouldn't be feeling like today is the start of a lifetime of pain. If there were no Jamie I would still be the shy sophomore who is obsessed with a boy band, who wears a contraption that prevents her spine from curving any more than it already has, who is made fun of by her peers and who had no clue what her future had in store. That girl's life was uncomplicated and easy because the only things she had to worry about was finals, finding clothing that would fit over the metal halo and whether or not the cafeteria would be serving day old pizza for lunch. That girl didn't know what it was to love someone completely only to lose them in the end. But is it really that easy to wish for a redo?

~35~

In a second I am going to open my eyes and this will all have

been a bad dream. When I wake up I will see the Dave Matthews

Band poster that I bought for Jamie a few weeks ago. I will smell the

Calvin Klein cologne he used to wear way too much of. I'll feel the

rigid fabric of the quilt his mother knitted for him, crumbled at the

foot of his bed. I will see his gorgeous eyes looking at me like I'm

the only person in the world worth looking at. I'll go to say

something but he'll stop me and whisper, "I love you April," and the

world will make sense again. This is what I will see and hear when I

open my eyes. I won't see the mundane wallpaper that has been

decorated with nonsensical portraits of woodland creatures. I won't

smell the musty scent of the molding carpet that probably hasn't

been washed in weeks. Jamie's loved ones won't be surrounding me

dressed in their darkest suits and dresses and clinging to damp

tissues. I am going to count to five and then open my eyes and this

lump in my throat will be gone. When I get down to one this whole day will be over and Jamie will be standing in front of me laughing

like this has all been a big joke.

Five…four…three…two…one.

I slowly open my eyes………..it's real, all of it. Jamie is

really gone.

Open caskets funerals are surreal. I'm sitting here staring at

my boyfriend who gave me the best six-months of my life and I

could swear he is just sleeping. But I know that his body is nothing

more than an empty shell now, like in my dream. The boy that I

loved disappeared the minute his heart stopped beating. When

Grandma Maggie died, although it was sudden, it wasn't entirely

unexpected. She had lived a long and wonderful life and I knew she

didn't have any regrets. When she died there was nothing we left

that was unsaid. When someone dies of natural causes you have time

to get things right but when someone dies suddenly time is working

against you and sometimes, like with me and Jamie, a lot is left

unsaid and you're forced to live the rest of your life replaying all of

the things you should have said when you had the chance.

The room shrinks as everyone gathers in front of the casket to say a prayer or to say goodbye to Jamie. It seems like everyone from school is here, even Mrs. Honor who always gave Jamie a hard time. She is here sobbing with the rest of us. Erik is holding Amber close to him as they wait their turn to say goodbye. They're both trying to be strong for the other. I don't know everyone here but I feel connected to all of them, even Liza who is kneeling beside the casket with her head bowed. She's whispering something but I can't make it out. As she rises to her feet again she turns around and mouths to me, "I'm so sorry." It is the first time that I don't want to punch her in the face. Although I am sure that once I go back to school in a few weeks I'll go right back to hating her and will look forward to seeing another one of her and Jeremy's famous fights. There are just some things that nothing, not even tragedy, can change.

"April," mom says, placing her hand on my knee, "it's time to say goodbye now."

This is it, the worst moment of my life. I'd wear a thousand braces for a million lifetimes to have Jamie back if only for a few minutes. I walk up to the casket and place my hands on Jamie's chest. I thought it would feel weird touching him but it feels like the only easy thing I'll do from now on. He looks peaceful and I swear he's smiling. I close my eyes and pretend he's standing in front of me. I can feel his hand brush the stray hairs out of my eyes the way he always did before he kissed me. I can feel the warmth of his touch and security of being wrapped in his arms.

"Tell me," I hear Jamie say. "Now is your chance. I'm here and I'm listening."

I lean in and push my lips against his ear and whisper, "You will never know how much I loved you Jamie" I say as tears pour down my face. "I am so sorry I let you go without resolving that ridiculous fight. Petty fights, that's not us. Thank you for showing me that this brace doesn't define me. Thank you for giving me the strength to look at myself and see past the cage I've been trapped in for the last two-and-a-half years. Thank you for making me feel beautiful and for choosing me. But most of all thank you for loving me."

I keep my eyes closed as I kiss his forehead.

"I love you April," I hear him say as I open my eyes. "I'll always be with you, even when you meet the Backstreet Boys this summer but I will haunt you if you fall in love with one of them." If he were standing here now I am sure he would make a joke like that. It wouldn't be Jamie if he didn't put a humorous spin on his own funeral.

I was so sure that I wouldn't be able to breathe today or have the strength to say goodbye but I've found a way to do it. Even in death, Jamie is giving me strength.

I had something that most people will never have; I had love…the real thing. I had that romantic-comedy movie kind of love. It was messy and sometimes it was so complicated I didn't think we'd make it, but despite the complications and mess what we had was real and it was ours and nothing, not even death could take that away from us.

~EPILOGUE~

It's been two months since I lost Jamie and although it's been hard I've managed to survive it. Things are different now though. I am stronger, more confident. This brace isn't who I am it is just a thing I have to deal with and I refuse to let it define me anymore. I have also been spending a lot of time with Mr. and Mrs. Clarke. It is comforting being around them and reminiscing about Jamie. My parents have also been spending time with them and every Friday we've been getting together for family dinners.

I finished the book and titled it, *Brace Yourself, Margo Hunch,* and I plan on submitting it to literary agencies in the next few weeks. I don't know where it will take me but I'm doing this for Jamie, because I know it's what he would want me to do and I owe it to him to at least try.

Two weeks after the funeral Liza broke up with Jeremy. She came up to me during lunch one day and told me how sorry she was that Jamie died. She even apologized for trying to steal him from me. I asked her why she and Jeremy broke up.

"I want what you and Jamie had," she said. "I realized that Jeremy would never love me the way Jamie loved you. I mean he really did." It was weird to hear that but it was also really flattering. I love that Jamie and I were the type of couple that others have been compared to.

Tonight is the concert in Portland. Amber volunteered to take Jamie's ticket and this time she promised I wouldn't have to drag her. I thought it would be too painful to be there without Jamie but he went through a lot of trouble to get these tickets and passes for me and I owe it to him to go. Besides if I don't go I know he'll be looking down on me from Heaven and cursing me. So I will go for him but I'll also go for me.

The day of Jamie's funeral Amber asked me if I regretted having met and fallen in love with Jamie. I didn't know what to say then but now I do. Jamie loved me in the way that made me want to live and enjoy every moment so that is what I am going to do. I am going to live for both of us and carry him with me until it's my turn to join him.

I will always regret the choices I made the night Jamie died. I used to tell Jamie that he was my everything but that night I treated him like he was nothing to me. No one could be for me what he was and is. Instead of telling him how thankful I was to have him in my life I ignored him when he reached out to me and now he's been taken from me; taken from this world too soon.

We had a developing and growing love and a story that will never have a conclusion -and THAT is the tragedy of loving Jamie Clarke; but do I regret meeting him and falling in love with him now that he's gone? Not for one second.

www.ingramcontent.com/pod-product-compliance
Lightning Source LLC
Chambersburg PA
CBHW061933170626
46813CB00006B/2383